THE END HOUSE

MICHAEL ROBERTSON, JR.

This book is a work of fiction. Names, characters, places, businesses, and incidents either are products of the author's imagination or are used in a fictitious manner. Any similarities to events or locales or persons, living or dead, is entirely coincidental and should be recognized as such. No part of this publication may be reproduced, stored or transmitted, in any form, or by any means (electronic, mechanical, etc.) without the prior written consent and permission of the author.

Copyright © 2022 Michael Robertson, Jr.

Cover Design Copyright © 2022 Jason Collins

ISBN: 978-1-7360939-9-3

DECLAN

I

1

The momentary flit of panic was over, thank God.

It had been brief, lasting only five or six seconds after Declan Scheider had awakened on the floor of the cold bedroom, but the anxiety that had filled his veins and caused his heart to thump hard and painfully in his chest and had made his breath hitch and sputter in choking gasps had been strong enough to send a fear-driven SOS message directly to the front of his mind: *You're going to die!*

Fear had grabbed Declan by the throat, the confusion of his unknown surroundings mixing with some underlying sense of worry and sadness and—*Guilt ... that's guilt, Deck*—had made it seem as though the bare plaster walls were laughing at him, the cracked ceiling staring down with a menacing grin, a *knowing* grin, like everyone was in on the secret but him. Declan had clawed at the blanket that was covering him, a green mothball-smelling thing that he had no memory of finding, no memory of ever owning, and kicked it off him. It tangled in his feet as he pushed himself from the uneven wooden floorboards while his heart still hammered and his lungs struggled for air, and he nearly went down again, but he caught himself with one hand on the windowsill and then stood straight, the pressure in his head giving him a brief sense of vertigo as his vision adjusted and he squinted against the morning sun rising over the trees in the distance.

He was on the second floor of the house, looking down at the front lawn that was all dead grass and a few lingering patches of melting snow. Big, maybe a whole acre surrounded by tall pines. Snowcapped tops of a distant mountain range rose above the tree line. Declan's eyes settled on the mountains, let their majesty take hold of him. He steadied himself against the edge of the window and watched as the sun heliographed off ice melting from treetops. His lungs started to feel like they might be up for breathing again, and he took ten slow and steady breaths, relishing the sweet air, feeling his heart begin to settle down.

Confident he wasn't going to pass out—*or die!*—Declan let his gaze fall from the mountains and look down to the yard again. A gravel driveway snaked from a slim opening in the tree line and fed toward the house. He followed the dark path with his eyes until he was nearly looking straight down, and when he saw the U-Haul parked with its nose almost nudging the porch railing, all at once the panic and fear and anxiety melted away like the ice on the tree limbs, and the memories felt as though they were literally rushing into him, pouring through a newly opened door to fill a space the way a crazed crowd of fans might rush through a venue's gate to try and get closest to the stage.

The memories filled that open space in his mind and then arranged themselves to tell their story, to set his mind at ease.

Oh, right, Declan thought, nodding to himself as he turned from the window, the heat of embarrassment flushing his cheeks. *This is our new home.*

2

Declan remembered it all clearly now, the truth of how he'd ended up in this house.

Their house.

He was glad that Norah and Knox weren't here yet. Norah would have been worried about him having the panic attack, would have asked him questions about whether he was still taking his medication, or if he'd made any effort yet to line up a new therapist now that they'd moved several states away from Dr. Pillsman's office.

Declan glanced over to where the tattered green blanket had landed after he'd kicked it free from his ankles, and found his old leather satchel leaned against the bare wall. His pills were in there, he knew, and, yes, he'd been taking them, even though he didn't really think he needed them anymore. He'd been doing great for years now. More specifically, he'd had no major incidents since the day Knox had been born. Parents always tell you how the day their child was born was the greatest day of their lives, and now Declan understood what they all meant. Something had shifted inside him when Knox had come into the world, as if a soothing balm had been applied to all Declan's internal wounds, a usurping happiness pushing out all the darkness that sometimes made him feel so crowded on the inside.

Declan was glad Knox wasn't here yet only because he wouldn't have wanted his outburst to scare his son. Daddy needed to be strong, not panicky and frightened all because of four new and unfamiliar walls.

He walked to his satchel and bent down to grab the strap, the floorboards creaking beneath his sneakers. The bag's leather surface was darkened with beautiful patina, telling a story of its own, and as Declan's fingers grasped the strap he smiled at the memory that jumped front and center in his mind: Norah gifting the satchel to him the day after he'd told her he'd finally sold his first book.

They'd gone out to dinner the night before to celebrate, and he'd never forget the way Norah had looked in the red dress, nor the lovemaking after. Plus, the feeling of accomplishment, the satisfaction at knowing that all his hard work and all their sacrifices had finally been worth it, was damn near euphoric in its own right.

Knox's birth had been the best day of Declan's life, but the day his agent had called to let him know the book had sold was a very close second. Closer than Declan would ever admit out loud to anyone.

He flipped open the bag's flap and pushed his laptop aside and felt around in the inner side pocket for his pill bottle. In the chaos of ink pens and charging cords and some loose change, the pill bottle was absent.

Hmm, Declan thought. *Must be in another suitcase. Or maybe in the U-Haul.*

A fresh image flooded his mind, one of him pulling up to the house late last night, the truck's headlights splashing across the front porch and first-floor windows. The windows, with some of their shutters broken and askew, had looked as though they were squinting against the light, like somebody had rudely awakened them. Declan had been driving all day and had been exhausted. He had no memory of even getting out of the truck and making his way to the bedroom, where he'd apparently passed out.

He shouldered the satchel and patted the front pocket of his jeans. Found his cell phone and called Norah. He should have done this last night, to let her know he'd made it to the house safely. She'd probably be pissed, and he wouldn't blame her. A lot can happen when you drive a big U-Haul full of furniture for...

How many miles was it? I don't remember.

Well, it had been a lot. Lots of miles and lots of hours and he felt like a major asshole for not calling.

Or did I? Maybe I did *call when I got here last night. I just don't remember.*

He shook his head. The long hours behind the wheel had clearly taken a toll on him. Suddenly he very much wished he could find his pills.

When he put the phone to his ear it didn't even ring, the call instantly being forwarded to Norah's voice mail, which was just the generic robotic female voice telling Declan to leave a message. Norah hated hearing the sound of her own recorded voice, a pet peeve of hers that Declan would never understand since he always found her voice to be lovely, and she'd never recorded a personalized voice mail greeting.

Shit, they must already be on the plane, Declan thought. He waited for the beep. "Hey, babe, it's me. Sorry I didn't call last night. Well, I don't think I called. I mean … sorry. It was … it was a long drive." He laughed. "Hell, I feel like I'm hungover, to be honest. I need to find some coffee. Anyway, I made it safe. I hope you had a good flight. Call me as soon as you land. I can't wait to see you all. Tell Knox I love him. Love you."

He ended the call and slid his phone back into his pocket.

3

Declan stepped out of the bedroom and found himself standing in a dark hallway running the width of the house. The door he'd come through was in the middle, and there were two doors to his left on either side of the hall, and one to his right. Dust motes floated lazily in the light spilling from the room behind him, but the hall was otherwise still and silent and full of deep shadows.

"Stuffy in here," Declan said, making his way to one of the doors to his left and opening it. Inside he found another bedroom nearly identical to the one he'd woken up in—same uneven flooring, same bare walls and cracked ceiling plaster. No green blanket here, but an empty glass bottle sat upright in the far corner, towering over a discarded aluminum can lying on its side, as though the bottle were a fighter who had emerged victorious. Declan walked to the corner and leaned down, examining the bottle. Found it was pineapple-flavored rum, and the empty can was a White Claw hard seltzer. He smiled, because these were exactly the kinds of fruity drinks Norah would choose, way too sweet for his own liking. Closer now, Declan saw the rum bottle wasn't completely empty, there was still maybe an ounce or two of the stuff left, and he had to stand up quickly and back away to fight off the absurd desire to pick the bottle up and gulp down the remains.

His head swam and his vision was peppered with black because of standing up too fast, and as Declan turned slowly around and closed his eyes and took another of those deep breaths, just like he'd done as he'd stared at the mountaintops in the room next to this one, he heard a girl laugh. His blood went cold, his heart jumping into his throat. Declan shot open his eyes and turned around—the laugh having come from behind him, from near the bottle.

There was nobody there, of course. Why would there be?

A gust of wind swooped from overtop the trees and sprinted across the yard, whistled across the front of the house, a soft and muffled scream.

Just the wind, Declan thought. *Come on, Deck, wake the fuck up.*

He needed coffee. Hell, he probably needed another few hours' sleep, but he knew there was too much to do. He needed to start unpacking what he could from the U-Haul and try to at least get Knox's crib upstairs and assembled before Norah and his son arrived. So, no rest for the weary. Coffee would have to do.

Or maybe something stronger? Something to take the edge off?

Declan stopped at the threshold of the bedroom. The thoughts had been his, spoken with his own internal voice, but he had no recollection of conjuring them into existence. He furrowed his brow at a sense of confusion that he found difficult to process, other than to think that the thoughts had tasted funny on his mind's tongue. As though they were not organic, but somehow modified or synthetic.

As he stepped out into the hallway again, Declan felt like the rum bottle was watching him.

Or maybe it was something else hidden in the corner of the room. Something that could watch … and laugh.

4

Declan opened the door across the hall from the rum room and found another bedroom, nothing on the floor in this one but a thin sheen of dust. The simple latticework in the old window tossed a tic-tac-toe board shadow toward him. He stepped forward and drew an X in the bottom right square with the toe of his sneaker. "Your move, house," he said and smiled to himself. He crossed the rest of the room and stepped up to the window and looked out.

The backyard was just as dead as the front. An old clothesline was off to the left, both poles leaning slightly, as if caught in a permanent windstorm, the line drooping. The remains of what looked like an old chicken coop long past its prime were an eyesore on the right side of the yard, and Declan mentally added dismantling and disposing of the ruins to his to-do list. He had no plans to raise chickens or, for that matter, any other animal. His only concern was raising his son. A challenge he was up and eager for, but one that he knew many had failed. Including his own father.

Declan pushed away the hint of his father's memory from his mind and instead let himself stare at what else the backyard had to offer—a big oval-shaped pond along the back of the property, complete with a small wooden dock and rowboat tied off, the small craft bobbing sleepily in the tranquil water. He smiled again, bigger this time, a fresh memory rushing into that room in his mind as the story became clear again. The memory of him and Norah looking at this home's listing on the website and seeing the picture of this pond and the dock and rowboat. The picture had been taken in late spring, and the trees and grass were all a brightly saturated green, the water tinted blue. It had seemed serene and perfect, a private oasis, their own slice of nature. They'd fantasized in those few seconds of staring at the picture on the laptop's screen about picnicking on the dock, their feet hanging over the edge, toes in the water, or taking a bottle of wine and getting into the boat and rowing out to the center of the pond and drinking and watching the sunset or staring up at the stars once night had fallen.

But of course, they'd have to be careful too. Because of Knox. Declan had heard enough stories of kids drowning in their own bathtubs when their parents had turned their backs for a couple seconds. The thought of Knox learning how to walk and then one day sneaking out the back door and stumbling into the pond was enough to give Declan heart palpitations and an ulcer combined. He'd have to ask Norah to do some research and find out how early you could teach a child to swim. Declan would make sure his son was prepared for everything the cruel world would throw at him, starting with the dangers lurking in his own backyard. Because if nothing else, Declan and Norah would make sure their son felt safe at home.

Declan left the window and checked to see if the house had made a move on the tic-tac-toe board on the floor, but of course there was only the faint outline of the X he'd etched through the dust. He reached out with his sneaker and traced an O in the middle square, getting hit with a flash of memory from his childhood, remembering the way his grandfather—his mother's father (Declan had never known his paternal grandparents)—used to play chess against himself, the board a permanent fixture in his grandparents' sunroom.

Declan smirked. "This is a long way from chess." And he thought maybe he'd buy a chess set for himself once they got the house settled. Teach Knox how to play when he got a little older. Declan hadn't played since high school but found he suddenly wanted to get back into it. Have a new hobby to exercise his mind. The peace and quiet of their new home and land would certainly be conducive to such a thing.

This place is going to be good for us, Declan thought, heading for the bedroom door.

A voice yelled from behind him, from outside, down in the yard. A high-pitched shriek that was a mixture of fear and glee. And then, right behind it, the unmistakable sound of something splashing into water.

Declan rushed to the window, his shoes smearing his incomplete tic-tac-toe game, and looked out toward the pond, certain he'd see kids horsing around.

But how? Nobody was there just a few seconds ago.

Plus, the water would have to be freezing. Swimming weather was still a few months away.

There was nobody there, of course, just like there'd been nobody laughing in the room with the rum bottle and just like the house had not made a move in the game.

But still, Declan squinted and stared at the pond, swearing to himself the water was rippling harder than it had been before, disturbed.

Wind, he thought again, turning to leave. *It'll take some time to get used to the sounds out here. A lot different than the city.*

5

The last door in the hallway, just before the stairs leading down to the first floor, was the bathroom. The old clawfoot tub didn't have a shower, and Declan knew that Norah would make it pricrity numero uno to renovate the bathroom. The tile flooring and baseboard around the tub were speckled with what Declan thought might be mold, and he tried to remember if the home inspection documents had cited anything about that. Nothing came to mind. Besides, he and Norah had known the place was going to be a major fixer-upper—they were prepared.

Declan stared down at the badly stained toilet bowl and did his business, having to jiggle the handle a bunch before the old porcelain throne finally choked its way through a flush. Pipes shuddered and groaned in the walls when Declan turned on the water at the sink, and after sputtering for a few seconds, the cold water started flowing nicely. It smelled faintly metallic, but otherwise alright, and Declan wondered if the pond out back was the source or if there was a well drilled somewhere on the property.

I really should have paid more attention to that home inspection, he thought.

He splashed a couple handfuls of water onto his face, the crisp cold like a wakeup slap, and then, after a moment's hesitation, he bent down and slurped a mouthful of the stuff. Again, a subtle metallic tang at the back of his throat, but otherwise alright. He got another mouthful and swished it around and then spat. He rubbed his tongue over his teeth and badly wanted to brush them, but he realized his toothbrush and toiletries must still be in his suitcase out in the U-Haul, left there when he had tumbled into the house exhausted last night.

With the thought of the U-Haul in the driveway came another hit of that guilt he'd experienced when he'd first woken up in his panicked and confused state—some wrongdoing nagging him at the back of his mind, reaching down and plucking strings in his gut.

I shouldn't have left them, he thought. *That's it. I left them to travel alone: a mother and a newborn.*

He remembered now, another memory rushing into that room in his mind. The brief argument he and Norah had had about whether Declan would drive a U-Haul himself to save money on having to hire a moving company. He'd argued that they could use the money they'd save to help with the home renovations, and even though Norah was clearly still unhappy about having to fly alone with their infant son, she'd eventually conceded his point. They weren't broke, but cash wasn't exactly overflowing either, so saving a chunk of change made sense.

Now, Declan wasn't so sure. He gripped the edges of the sink and stared into the dirty mirror above it. He was thirty-one, his brown hair thinning, a lot more gray in the stubble on his cheeks and chin than there'd been even just last year. It was probably only because of the long drive and the crummy night's sleep, but looking in the mirror right then, seeing the dark bags under his eyes, Declan thought he looked like shit. He looked haunted.

He wondered if deciding whether to let his wife and son travel alone was one of his first tests as a new father.

If it was, he had failed.

There was a quick moment while Declan looked in the mirror at his tired and strained eyes where he realized he hated himself, was undeserving of Norah and unfit to raise his son and certainly not a man who would be able to sustain his family's fresh start here at their new home.

Don't let an unknown future spoil the present. That was Dr. Pillsman's voice in his head, a mantra that had become commonplace in their discussions. It was a flaw of Declan's, he knew that, letting his worry and anxiety set up roadblocks in his mind, cordoning off the path to happiness ahead. He and the doctor had spent many hours discussing Declan's inability to live in the moment, trying to get Declan to learn to focus on what was right in front of him instead of fearing the future ... or dwelling on the past.

"What is this moment?" Declan asked himself in the mirror. "What is today?"

He stared at himself for a few seconds, part of him

wishing that the version of himself in the mirror might actually answer for itself, but when the mirror version only remained as anticipatory as Declan himself, Declan swallowed down the lump in his throat and said, "Today is a happy day. Today is the first day in our new house. Norah and Knox will be here soon and we can start our life together. We're happy now, and we'll be happy for a long time to come."

He left the bathroom and started down the stairs. Stopped three steps from the bottom when the aroma of freshly brewed coffee and cooked bacon hit him. Heard what sounded like somebody scraping a spatula across a pan.

Norah.

That was Declan's first thought. Somehow their flight had gotten in early and she'd snuck into the house to surprise him with breakfast together in their new home. God, how he loved her. She was always doing little things like this, always making him feel special.

I don't deserve her, he thought, that guilt creeping up his spine again. Norah had to be exhausted and irritable after the long flight and the added stress of traveling alone with an infant, yet here she was, cooking them breakfast and probably eager and ready to head outside and start the arduous unloading of the U-Haul.

But, no, he wouldn't let her. She needed to rest. Declan would get their bed upstairs and assembled and tell her to take as long of a nap as she needed. He'd be just fine unloading on his own and would take care of Knox in the process.

Because I will be better, he thought. *I will be the husband and father those two deserve.*

Declan smiled and took the last three steps down to the foyer with a bit of forced pep in his step, rounded the banister and went down the short hallway to the kitchen at the back of the house.

The moment he stepped through the entryway, the smells of coffee and bacon vanished, and of course the kitchen was empty.

6

Declan knew he was in desperate need of caffeine. That much was certain.

What he had seen looking back at him in the mirror should have been enough to let him know he was exhausted and running on fumes, but now for the third time since he'd woken up his brain had played a trick on him. No one had laughed, there'd been nobody horseplaying in the pond, and of course, with him being all alone in the house, it was impossible that somebody would have been cooking bacon and brewing coffee.

With the fantasy wiped away the second he'd stepped into the kitchen, Declan realized how absurd the idea was that Norah and Knox would be here already. She would have let him know if their flight's schedule had changed, and Declan would have seen their rental car parked in the driveway earlier when he'd looked out the window. He remembered now, making the reservation online for their car, ticking the box for the car seat add-on for Knox. He remembered hoping that the rental car agency would have the car seat installed ahead of time; that way Norah wouldn't have to do it herself. Alone.

Better. I've got to be better.

His guilt and his exhaustion were mixing together to create a cocktail of self-loathing and delusion, and this only depressed Declan more. He truly believed he'd been doing well on his own, without the need for his pills, and didn't want to have to fall back on them now.

I'll be better when they get here, he thought. *When we're all here as a family and make this house our home, I'll be better.*

Declan closed his eyes and took a deep breath. Held it in and counted to ten before letting it out. "Live in the moment," he said to the kitchen walls. "Be present."

An ancient beige refrigerator sat silently in the corner, unplugged with its cord lying limp beside it. The door was open a crack, and Declan saw a family of dead flies piled on the bottom shelf. To the left of the fridge, cut out between it and the stove, the back door had a long rectangular window in its middle, smeared and grimy now, but Declan was happy to see that, once it was clean, one would be able to sit at the square wooden breakfast table and look straight out to the pond. It would be a perfect place to have your morning cup of coffee.

Speaking of which…

Declan wasn't sure what he was thinking, expecting to find coffee in the empty kitchen, but something at the back of his brain encouraged him to check anyway. If he lucked out, it would save him the time and hassle of having to drive the big and unwieldy U-Haul into town in search of a café. He'd driven that thing enough for one lifetime.

His sneaky intuition paid off, because after opening and closing most of the cabinets above the counter, at first finding only more dead flies and lots of mouse droppings —*Gonna have to get some traps*—the last cabinet proved fruitful. An old can of instant coffee sat alone on the bottom shelf. Next to it were two tin coffee mugs that looked like something people might use when they went camping, dented and, like most everything else Declan had come across in the house, misted with the sheen of dust. He pulled down the can of instant coffee and one of the mugs and then looked back to the stove. There was an old kettle meant to look like a rooster on one of the burners.

There might be a God after all, Declan thought.

He grabbed the kettle and walked over to the sink, a single deep basin that reminded Declan more of a slop sink you might find in a basement or garage than in a kitchen. He tried to remember what year the listing had said the house had been built, but couldn't recall. He turned on the cold tap and heard more rumbling and groaning from the pipes in the wall, louder here than in the bathroom upstairs. The sink literally vibrated for a couple seconds right before the water began to flow. Unlike in the bathroom, the water here started out a little cloudy, but after a loud gurgle and another shudder from a pipe somewhere, it cleared up. Declan got another whiff of that faintly metallic scent as he first rinsed the kettle out and then filled it with water before turning off the tap.

Back at the stove, he set the kettle on the burner and

tried to turn it on with the knob. This caused a nearly inaudible hiss.

Gas, Declan remembered. *I'll have to call the gas company and have them come check everything out. Get on their refill schedule.* There was a dusty box of long-stemmed matches sitting atop the stove, and Declan scratched one against the rough side of the box and it lit on the first try. He'd never worked a gas stove before, so he cautiously stepped backward, stretching his arm out, using his free hand to shield his face as he gingerly eased the lit match into the burner.

There was only a soft *whoosh* as the burner sparked to life, and thankfully no explosion. Pleased with himself, Declan tossed the match into the big basin sink and then went to take a look at the rest of the downstairs of the house while he waited for his water to boil.

That was when he saw the book for the first time.

7

A small bathroom was under the stairs, the ceiling sloping enough that at six foot two, Declan had to duck down a little to keep from hitting his head when standing in front of the toilet. He turned on the tap at the sink and let it run. The mirror above the sink had a series of cracks in the upper corner, but that would be easy to replace. He flushed the toilet and watched the water swirl away and then refill, just to make sure everything was in working order. Or at least close enough to working order that he could push any repairs further down his to-do list.

There were two other rooms on the ground floor of the

old house, wide-open entryways, one with ornate crown molding and trim that looked decidedly out of place with the rest of the architecture. The room to the right of the stairs must have been a dining room for the previous owners, because there was a tarnished silver chandelier hanging from the center of the ceiling, cobwebs draping it like a Halloween decoration, and an oak china cabinet sat empty in one corner with a crack cutting across the glass in one of its doors. Declan smiled at the thought of buying a nice dining table to put under the chandelier and then having big family Thanksgiving and Christmas dinners here. They'd invite Norah's parents, and maybe even her brother, Jordan, and his family if she was up for it—they had a bit of a rocky relationship, Norah and her bro, mostly because Jordan was a successful financial advisor for some big-deal firm in New York, and he looked down on his sister marrying, quote, *an artist with no stable future.*

The words had stung a little when Declan had heard them, but he didn't dwell on it. It was the sort of thing you got used to when you spent your whole life telling people you were a writer. Came with the territory. But Norah had taken offense for him, and had essentially told Jordan to fuck off with his slick suits and overpriced haircuts. She also might have asked Jordan's wife, Sydney, what it was like to have sex with the expensive cardboard box that was her brother, and if Sydney had to quote the day's Dow Jones Industrial Average to get Jordan's cock hard.

Yeah ... it was rocky. But Declan told Norah she was lucky to at least have a family that loved her, unlike him.

Declan left the dining room and crossed in front of the

stairs and stopped just short of the entryway to the other room, taking a moment to inspect the carved pattern in the crown molding and trim all around the entryway. It was incredibly detailed and elegant, somewhat unfitting for such a place, depicting what looked like leaves and tree branches. Declan wondered if Norah would like it or want to replace it but figured that would be a project well down on his list.

This was the living room, empty except for a hideous green couch pushed against the lefthand wall, directly beneath a front window. Even in the morning light filling the room, the couch's dull pea-colored fabric reminded Declan of the stuff the little girl had spit up in *The Exorcist*, and decided that from today forward the couch's name would be Regan.

People name boats and cars all the time, Declan thought as he moved across the room toward the small fireplace built into the far wall on the side of the house. *So why can't I name a couch?*

The name—and the couch—wouldn't last long anyway. He knew Norah would take one look at the ugly thing and probably ask him to take it outside and burn it. Besides, who knew how long the thing had been here? He thought of the mouse droppings he'd seen in the kitchen cabinets and wondered what he might find if he were to lift those ugly green cushions.

Declan reached the fireplace and leaned down to get a closer look, bracing himself against the mantel. He nudged the knee-height stand holding deep-black iron tools—a mini-shovel, brush, set of tongs, and fire poker—and the group gently clanged together as they swayed, sounding like a wind chime. Declan watched and listened until they fell still and silent again. The fireplace was made of once-red brick, now mostly charred from a lifetime of flames, painted with ash the color of charcoal gray that deepened to a heavy black in the center. The remnants of previous fires—ashes and chunks of wood and debris—were scattered across the brick, and in this mess something caught Declan's eye. He squinted and leaned down even further, his head looking as though the fireplace was swallowing it, and reached out a cautious index finger to brush some of the ash aside and pluck free what he'd noticed. He held the small square of paper up into the light.

"Is that ... money?" he asked nobody.

What Declan held pinched between his thumb and index finger looked like a scorched piece of United States paper currency. It was impossible to tell what denomination the bill had once been, but also impossible to deny that Declan was surely holding what was left of destroyed cash.

Why would somebody burn money?

Before he could ponder the question any further, the book caught his eye.

Declan had stood and faced the front windows when he'd examined the small scrap of cash, and now from the corner of his eye, the black book seemed to jump out at him. He turned, letting the piece of paper flutter from his hand to the floor, and at first he thought that the book lying on its side atop the mantel was a Bible. It had the look—worn black leather with dark red stitching, and what looked like gold text etched into the top cover. Declan reached for the book and pulled it from the mantel, and in that one or two seconds before the piercing whistle from the teakettle in the kitchen screamed and echoed through the downstairs, causing Declan to jump back and drop the book, he would have sworn that those gold-etched letters on the cover had shifted and moved, vanished and reappeared anew. They had formed a single word.

DECLAN

The combination of seeing his name, plus the jolt of adrenaline from the surprise of the kettle's whistle, had given Declan's heart a start. He placed a hand on his chest and took another of those deep breaths and forced himself to laugh at his own skittishness.

The book had landed facedown next to the charred scrap of cash, and Declan eyed it suspiciously for a few seconds before he bent down and snatched it from the floor, flipping the smooth leather over in his hands to look at his name on the front cover.

But there was nothing on the other side of the book. Both sides were now blank, no trace of the existence of any gold lettering. He turned the book over two more times in his hands, then walked over to the front window by Regan and held the book in the sunlight, hoping to catch a glint or outline or ... anything to let him know that what he'd seen was real.

Confusion and, he had to admit, for the first time, a real sense of worry draped over him like a cloak. The kettle's whistle seemed to grow louder the longer Declan stood staring at the blank cover of the black leather book, bathed in sunlight, louder until it felt as though the whistle was boring into his brain, a siren blasting a warning.

Declan tossed the book onto Regan, where it bounced once off a green cushion and settled in a plume of dust. It was only as Declan reached the kitchen and pulled the kettle from the stove top that he realized he hadn't even peeked inside the book to see what filled its pages.

8

A plastic teaspoon scoop was inside the old instant coffee can, and Declan filled it once and brought it to his nose for a sniff. He had no idea how old the coffee was, or if instant coffee could even expire, but as he inhaled the aroma coming from the scoop, all he could think was *Smells like coffee to me*, and he shrugged and dumped three heaping scoopfuls into the tin mug and then filled it with the steaming water from the kettle. He used the scoop to stir it all until the grounds dissolved, and then, for another questioning second or two, he held the mug in front of his lips and watched as the steam floated up from it. He took a small, cautious sip.

"*Shit*, that's hot!" He pulled his head back but miraculously kept his hand steady, not spilling a single drop. He licked his lips, his eyes watering from the liquid burning down his throat. *Hot, but...*

He blew across the top of the mug for a few seconds and then took another sip, this one bigger than before. His eyes widened and he stood up straighter and smiled. *But damn that's good!*

Declan looked down into the mug, at the murky brown

liquid that had just lit up his taste buds, and then over to the counter where the can sat, which appeared to be looking back at him with a sense of pride. He was astounded—and admittedly skeptical—to think that a dusty old can of *instant* coffee long forgotten in an empty house had just produced what might be the best cup of joe Declan had ever tasted.

Declan laughed and took another sip, which was just as bold and satisfying as the last.

"I'll be damned." He took another glance at the can on the counter, hoping he could find more of the stuff on his first grocery run into town. He might never drink another brand of coffee again.

From the front of the house, the *whooshing* of another gust of wind crashing down across the yard from over the mountaintops bounded toward Declan like an approaching train. It hit the house with a *thud*, like a giant's kick, and then wailed a high-pitched note as it split in two and sprinted around the sides of the house. Declan listened to the noise and tried to pull out the sounds that might have been the laugh he had heard upstairs, or the scream and the splash. But before he could think too much about it, the back door between the unplugged fridge and the stove popped open, floating slowly on silent hinges.

Declan watched as the door crept open, cold air rushing in at him from the backyard. The door unhurriedly continued on its path until it came to rest against the side of the fridge with a soft kiss. The rustling of tree branches and the skittering of fallen leaves and the distant chirping of birds filled the kitchen with a song. The moment had frozen Declan in place, his blood temporarily going cold as the door had opened itself, the mug of perfect coffee held partway to his lips, halted mid-sip.

Finally, he cleared his throat, took a sip of coffee, and said, "Guess fixing that door latch needs to go on the to-do list." Then he walked outside to explore the backyard, hesitating for only a second before grabbing the doorknob and pulling the door closed behind him.

9

The winter air carried a bite that cut through Declan's sweatshirt and jeans, but the coffee was warming him from the inside out and the sun climbing into the sky helped soothe the chill. Crunching softly under his sneakers, the grass in the backyard was stiff and dead, waiting to thaw. The ground was hard now, but Declan wondered how fertile the soil might be once things warmed up, if he and Norah could start a garden back here. Tomatoes and cukes and squash, for starters. The image of Norah in a sundress and flip-flops out here in the yard, pulling a ripened harvest from the vines while little Knox played in the dirt with a toy shovel and pail, made Declan's heart soar. Maybe they could build a nice back patio and put out a table and big umbrella and Declan could sit in the shade with his laptop and write his next book while looking out to the pond and the trees and letting the vastness of nature inspire.

Lord knows I need some inspiration, Declan thought as he gave the decrepit chicken coop a glance and then headed for the wooden dock that jutted a short way into the pond. *I need something.*

It was true, his last book from three years ago had yet to earn out his advance, being met with mediocre reviews and even worse sales. He'd self-published a collection of short stories he'd worked on over the years, and that brought in a surprising amount of cash each month, but it certainly wasn't enough to live on forever. His agent, God bless her, still had faith in him, but faith would only go so far without a new book to try and sell to publishers.

They're waiting for it, Declan. Forget the last book. Every author has a dud now and then.

That was what she'd told him during their last phone call. Declan hadn't called or emailed her since, because the longer he could go without actually admitting the truth to somebody, the better.

He wasn't sure he even had another book in him. His creative well, it seemed, had run dry. And if there was no book, there was no advance. With no advance, and diminishing royalty checks from his first two books (which *had* earned out), he was only a few bad months away from having to get a job to support his family. Which he would do, of course he would. He'd do whatever it took to give Norah and Knox everything they'd ever want. But inside his heart, deep in his soul, Declan was sickened and embarrassed by the notion that he'd failed at being the only thing he'd ever wanted to be—a writer. Admitting to yourself that you're not good enough is never easy. It's even harder admitting it to those you love.

Declan stepped onto the dock and had to stop, another fleeting feeling of vertigo grabbing him as the water gently rippling beneath him caused the optical illusion of the dock swaying back and forth. Once he had his bearings, Declan walked to the end of the dock and looked out over the water, feeling the sun on his back, which tossed his shadow across the pond, and taking another glorious sip of coffee. He smacked his lips in satisfaction and breathed in the fresh mountain air, cool in his lungs, revitalizing. He stood that way for a long time, the world around him melting away, not even realizing how much time had passed until he lifted the tin mug to his lips for another sip of coffee and found it empty, and then looked down at the water and saw that his shadow had shifted to a hard slant as the sun had crawled across the sky.

He meant to turn around and head back to the house, thinking he'd make some more coffee and then gear up to begin unloading the U-Haul. But even though he'd made that decision, even though his brain was telling his legs to pivot and do a 180 to head back to the yard and then eventually to the house, Declan found himself rooted in place. His legs didn't move, didn't obey the signals being sent from his brain, his nerves and muscles unresponsive. The decision felt held captive, locked away and ignored no matter how loudly it screamed and pounded against the door. It was replaced with a new desire, a freshly drawn plan of action. Declan blinked, and he was no longer in himself. Instead, he was standing back on the shore on the far side of the pond, furthest from the house. He was looking back across the water to the dock, saw himself standing on the edge, coffee mug still in hand.

And then the Declan on the dock stepped off the edge and fell into the water, barely making a splash.

Declan blinked again and he was back on the dock, standing exactly where he'd been. He gasped and jumped back, the wooden boards sounding hollow beneath his footfalls. He coughed as his heart rose into his throat, and his lungs seemed to be begging for air. He sucked in deep breaths and tried to calm himself, closing his eyes and counting, just like Dr. Pillsman had taught him.

With his heart and breathing settled again, Declan inched his way forward to the edge of the dock, a strange sense of curiosity propelling him. He toed the edge and leaned forward, peering down into the water.

Fear and panic seized him with icy talons that dug into his flesh. Declan screamed and this time he didn't just jump back, he fell, losing his balance and going down hard, the coffee mug *tink-tink-tinking* away from him and then rolling off the side of the dock, lost. Declan scrambled to his feet and then ran back toward the house.

When he'd looked over the edge of the dock, he'd seen himself beneath the water's surface, screaming and fighting as blackened and rotting hands reached up from the depths and pulled him down.

10

Declan was surprised at how quickly his fear had dissipated. In that moment when he'd first glimpsed himself beneath the water struggling against monstrous hands, the bubbles of a silent scream billowing from his gaping mouth, Declan had been certain he'd stepped into a nightmare from which he'd never wake up. It was a new, primal sense of fear that had instantly sparked to life inside him, a great bonfire of terror that would never be extinguished. His body had reacted the only way it could fathom—it had run away.

Declan sprinted across the yard with his heartbeat pounding in his ears and his chest feeling like it would burst open at any moment, the sense of some cosmic shift in his understanding of reality weighing down his thoughts, dominating his consciousness.

But then Declan had reached the house. He'd grabbed the doorknob and—even though for an instant, that bonfire in his gut had told him the door would be locked and he'd turn around and look back to the pond and would see those hands of rotting flesh reaching up and gripping the dock to pull themselves out of the water and come for him—was relieved to find that it turned easily and the door swung open as silently as it had before. As soon as he crossed the threshold and slammed the door behind him, he started to feel better. The nightmare began to fade, the way they always did in the mornings after you'd opened your eyes and let the real world begin to take shape again. He turned and pressed his forehead against the door's dirty glass and closed his eyes, hearing Dr. Pillsman's voice in his head as he took deep breaths again and counted. The air inside the house smelled and tasted different now that Declan had been outside in nature—industrial, almost. Tinged with dust and mildew and a staleness born of abandonment.

After counting to ten, Declan opened his eyes and looked out across the yard. The pond was still and the sun had climbed higher into the sky, casting an amber sheen over the stiffened grass, sparking off the occasional ripple of water. The scene was again beautiful, serene.

The bonfire of terror fizzled out, and as rational thought began to trickle back into Declan's mind, he relaxed.

Stress, he told himself. *You're exhausted, and you're stressed, and ... shit, Deck, admit it, you're fucking terrified of failing them. But, hey, that's natural, right? Every husband and father worth a damn feels that way, right?*

The thought of Norah and Knox helped a smile spread across Declan's lips as he continued to stare at the pond. The irony wasn't lost on him—the fact that his wife and son could both be the cause of so much joy and such a sense of purpose and also make him feel like he was being eaten alive from the inside out.

"Live in the moment," Declan said, his breath fogging the glass. "Be present."

Presently, he decided, he wanted more coffee.

He set another kettle to boil and rinsed out the other tin mug, wondering if the mug he'd dropped out on the dock was floating atop the pond's surface right now, a vessel for some small insect or rodent to sail the high seas, or if it had hit the water and sunk down into the darkness where

(Where those hands are waiting to snatch it)

he'd never be able to find it again.

The kettle began to whistle while Declan stood with his arms crossed, watching it, lost in the depths of his own mind. He added water to the mug and stirred in the wonderful instant coffee—*four* scoops this time—and blew across the brim, finding himself impatient for the first sip. When the liquid passed his lips and the flavor burst on his tongue, the only thought or emotion that could come to mind to describe the moment was *bliss*.

Something else was hidden beneath that bliss, though. Something below the surface, lost in the blackness of unknown and forgotten. Declan could hear it, faintly—or maybe he was just imagining it. A tiny voice, *his* voice, begging him...

Pills, Declan thought. *It's time. I need my medication.*

He hated to have the thought, but he couldn't afford to ignore it any longer. He was pretty sure that all his, shall we say, *unusual* experiences this morning were because of his lack of sleep—*and food*, he realized—and his stress and worry, plus the unfamiliarity of his new home and environment, but Declan understood that with Norah and Knox only a few hours away from arriving, he didn't want to take any chances that these experiences might be caused by something else—the part of him that was broken.

Dr. Pillsman wouldn't like Declan using that word —*broken*—but since Declan wasn't likely to ever see the good doctor again—fuck it.

U-Haul, Declan remembered. The pills hadn't been in his satchel, so he figured he had probably left them in the U-Haul.

He turned to head out to the front yard to check the truck's cabin for his pill bottle but never even took his first step.

The black book with the red stitching, the book that Declan clearly remembered tossing onto Regan and leaving there when he'd come to make his first cup of coffee, was sitting on the wooden breakfast table.

11

Declan, with his brain once again frozen in the icy chill of confusion, remained where he was, just in front of the kitchen counter, and stared at the black book on the table. After thirty seconds that seemed to tick by as slowly as if they were also having to thaw themselves from ice, Declan did the only thing he could think to do in that moment. He called out, "Hello?"

His voice was surprisingly loud, booming through the downstairs hallway, invading the dining and living rooms. Declan waited, holding his breath and listening for any signs of life: the shuffling of feet, a car engine purring as tires spun over the gravel driveway, the creak of a floorboard, or—worst case or best case, he wasn't so sure which—a voice answering back.

There was nothing. If anything, the house now seemed quieter than before, as if somebody had shut off the ambient noise machine and turned down the volume on the songs of nature playing out in the yard.

Declan didn't bother calling out again. He knew he was alone, understood it with a clear certainty he could not explain. He took a sip of coffee, and the stuff warmed his insides and got his legs moving. As he stepped across the kitchen floor and reached the breakfast table, positioning himself behind the chair that faced the back door—the very chair in which Declan had imagined himself spending his mornings, enjoying his coffee and the view of the yard and pond—he realized that he no longer harbored any fear, only curiosity. Curiosity ... and a slightly unsettling sense of questioning.

He was curious as to how the book had ended up on the kitchen table, because he had a vivid memory of finding the book in the living room atop the mantel and, after briefly examining it, tossing it onto the ugly green couch he'd named.

But he was now questioning whether that was actually what had happened. Because, aside from that memory, Declan's mind also housed the incredibly detailed and lived-in memories of watching himself step off the dock and into the pond, and another of peering into the water and watching monsters drag him away as he fought and screamed. And those two things, he knew, after returning to the house and calming down, were impossible and had not occurred.

Except in my head, he thought. *Stress-induced delusions.*

So maybe, now that he was looking at things in the rational light again, the memory of examining the book—*My name ... I thought it had my name on the front*—and tossing it onto Regan, where it had disturbed the dust and bounced a single time on the cushion, was the same sort of memory as the dock and those blackened and rotting hands.

I made it up, Declan thought. *I must have carried the book in here with me when the kettle started to whistle and I set the book on the table and just ... forgot about it until now.*

He chuckled to himself and shook his head. *Maybe I'll get that new book written easier than I thought*, he considered. *My imagination is clearly looking for ways to flex its muscles.*

With this fresh perspective enabling Declan to explain

away any negativity, allowing him to feel safe again, he shrugged and pulled out the chair and sat at the table, taking another sip of coffee before setting his mug down and then picking up the book with hands. As he tilted the book toward him, the glint of gold lettering caught his eye.

What? But ... no ... I was just...

He couldn't explain it but found he also couldn't quite trust his own recollection at this point. What he *thought* he knew was that just moments ago he'd been standing over the table and looking down at that book, with its soft black leather and red stitching along the spine and edges, and the cover had definitely been blank.

Just like it was in the living room before I tossed it onto Regan.

If you tossed, you mean...

Whatever had happened or not happened in the living room, right now Declan lifted the book higher, bringing it closer to his face for a better look, and then pulled it back and ran his finger over the etched gold lettering.

The letters were real. He could see them with his own two eyes, and he could feel the texture of them beneath his finger. But this time they didn't spell his name. Instead, they offered another.

IVAN

Declan looked at the name and wondered who the man was. Wondered if the word was a label of ownership, the title of a piece of work, or if maybe Ivan was the author of whatever story filled the book's pages.

There was only one way to find out.

Declan took another sip of coffee, settled into the chair, and flipped open the book's cover. There was no title page, no copyright page. The words started immediately in tiny, single-spaced type.

Ivan figured his brother was dead...

IVAN

1

Ivan figured his brother was dead.

"You think he's alright?" Jessica asked from the Dodge Charger's passenger seat. "You think they killed him?"

Those were the first words either of them had spoken since Ivan had peeled rubber in the gas station parking lot and shot the Charger onto the darkened two-lane highway like a startled bat taking flight in the night, leaving their brother, the cops, and—the object that was of more concern to Ivan than his fallen sibling—the *cash* behind.

"Don't know," Ivan lied to his sister. "Didn't see what happened real good."

In the dim glow from the Charger's dash, Ivan watched in his peripheral as Jessica cast a sideways glance at him, a flicker of doubt surely dancing across the front of her mind.

But then she turned and faced forward again, looking out

at the desolate highway, the base of the mountains taking shape in the distance like great slumbering beasts.

Ivan had seen what had happened. He'd seen it just fine. The cop's bullet had hit high up on Jonas's chest, from what Ivan could tell, and the second bullet had punched into Jonas's neck, blood spraying across the cashier's face. Ivan had only caught a glimpse of the moment when everything had happened, because after he'd fired his own gun, Ivan had known everything had officially gone to shit and he and Jessica would have to get the fuck out of there fast. Jonas was on his own—dead or alive.

"If he's alive, you think he'll rat us out?" Jessica asked, but Ivan could tell she already knew the answer.

"Fuck no," Ivan said, slowing the car as the trees began to encroach on both sides of the road, the mountain land opening its arms to envelop them. Though, truth be told, Ivan wasn't so sure his little bro wouldn't have squealed like a pig and told the police anything they wanted to know the moment any amount of pressure was applied. Jonas would probably offer Ivan and Jessica up on a silver fucking platter if it would buy him a lesser sentence or any sort of immunity.

Jonas had always been the weak one, the timid and anxious one. Was always telling Ivan and Jessica how they could all have a better life together if they would just put their heads together and work toward a common goal—one that was *legal*, and didn't require guns and masks and schemes and lies and drugs.

Delusional, Ivan always thought when he would listen to Jonas's plans for them. *He doesn't understand who we are, where we come from. People like us don't get the type of life he* wants. *The Universe deals the cards and you play what you get. Jonas thinks he has pocket aces when all we're really holding is a low pair—and we're lucky to have that.*

Once into the trees, the moonlight vanished and the inside of the car grew darker, and it started to feel stuffy —*Like a coffin*, Ivan thought. He cracked the front windows, and the noise of the warm summer air rushing through the gaps caused Jessica to jump. "*Christ*, Ivan. You could have fucking warned me!" She shot her left arm out and backhanded him across the chest. She was strong, and the blow did sort of hurt, but Ivan smiled.

"Don't be so damn jumpy."

"Fuck you. How are you so calm right now?"

Ivan shrugged and slowed the car even more to take a curve in the road. "It's over. We made it out alive, and"—he pointed up to the rearview mirror—"nobody's chasing us. In fact, we haven't seen a single car since we left the gas station. We're good."

He caught a shift in her posture again, knowing she was giving him another of those looks. "You don't believe that. You *know* better than that, Ivan. They're going to be looking for us. The gas station is going to have security footage of us, of the car." She paused and took a breath, calming herself. The air whispered through the Charger's cabin as Ivan steered through another bend in the road, the sound of the engine and the tires humming over asphalt echoing back at them off the trees. "Why did you have to fucking shoot that cop? *Why?* I don't know much, but one thing I do know is that when you shoot a cop, you become public enemy number one real fucking quick."

Ivan said nothing. Pressed down on the accelerator and the Charger leapt forward into a straight stretch. When he noticed that Jessica was not turning her gaze away from him, he finally sighed and shrugged again and said, "I thought it would help. I thought it would cause a diversion and Jonas could make a run for it."

Maybe Jessica bought it, maybe she didn't. Either way, after another ten seconds Ivan saw his sister face forward and slump down into her seat. "Where are we even going?" she asked, capitulation lacing her voice.

Ivan cleared his throat, happy to feel in charge again, to be making the plans and moving on. "I think the interstate runs by the town on the other side of the mountains. We can jump on there and head south. Hell, we can keep going till we hit Florida if you want."

He caught the faint movement of Jessica nodding. "Why south?"

His answer came out of his mouth so fast and honest it surprised him. "Because north will take us home, and right now, after tonight, I'm not sure I ever want to see home again."

Jessica's lighter sparked in the dark, and she took a long drag on a cigarette. Blew the smoke out the crack in the window. "I hear that," she said. "It's not like home's ever done anything for us."

Ivan nodded. "Nothing but a low pair."

"What?"

"Nothing."

Headlights rounded another bend up ahead of them, and the twin beams came speeding upon the Charger fast. On instinct, Ivan tapped the brakes, gently pulled the Charger closer to the right side of the road.

"Shit, they're flying," Jessica said, sitting up in the seat, the amber tip of the cigarette bobbing up and down on her lips as she talked.

Ivan felt his heart start to beat faster, an inkling of panic threatening to take hold. The headlights of the approaching car bore down on them, and then the vehicle's form began to take shape, carved out of the blinding light, and that was when Ivan saw it—the light bar mounted atop the speeding car.

It was a police cruiser.

2

"Oh fuck, is that a cop?" Jessica pushed herself up so high in the passenger seat her head touched the ceiling.

"Yes," Ivan said. "Sit down and shut up." His voice was ice-cold, and he stared into the rearview after the police cruiser had blown past them, holding his breath while he waited for the cruiser's brake lights to tint the night blood red and those blue lights to pop on and begin to flash.

Then Ivan's heart leapt into his throat, because after five or so seconds, the cruiser's brake lights *did* light up the road and the trees, and Ivan's foot was a millisecond away from smashing the Charger's gas pedal to the floor and beginning the inevitable highspeed chase. Which he knew could only end one way—because the last time he'd gotten out, Ivan had made a promise to himself that he'd rather die than ever go back to prison.

But then the cruiser's headlights and brake lights completely vanished, and Ivan realized the car had only slowed down enough to take one of the many curves in the road.

Jessica, who'd been watching in her side mirror, slumped into her seat again. "*Fuck.* I thought we were done."

"We've got to get off the road," Ivan said with a sudden burst of fresh inspiration, a new plan taking shape in his mind. "Fuck going south. We're going to hide out right here, right under their fucking noses. They won't expect us to stay put. Running is exactly what they want us to do, so they can set up their traps and catch us."

Jessica didn't say anything, which annoyed Ivan. "What?" he said. "You don't trust me now?"

There was a long hesitation, and Ivan was about to stop the car and tell his sister that if she didn't trust him, if she wanted to blame him for what had happened, she could get right the fuck out of his car and figure shit out on her own. But before he had to do that, Jessica answered, her voice small and not entirely convincing. "I do," she said. "Of course I trust you."

Ivan nodded. "Good. You know I'll always look out for you. And—hey, look there!" He slowed the car so fast that Jessica dropped her cigarette and scrambled to pick it up from the floorboard. Ivan pointed to a barely visible clearing in the trees to their left, the start of a gravel road that disappeared into the darkness. A path to nowhere.

Or a path to everywhere, Ivan thought.

"What?" Jessica said, leaning forward and peering over the dash. "A service road?"

Ivan shook his head. "I don't think so."

Jessica didn't seem to care. "So what, then?" She tossed her cigarette out the crack in the window.

"Might be a place to hide, at least for tonight."

As Ivan said the words, he found he was overcome with a great sense of desire, a longing to drive down this mysterious gravel road at the base of the mountains. Like it was calling his name, singing to him, telling him everything would be alright if he would only listen.

Compelled, Ivan thought. *That's the smarty-farty word Jonas would use. I feel* compelled.

"What do you think?" he asked Jessica.

"I think I've seen enough cops for one night," she said. "So yeah, fuck it. Let's see what's down there."

Ivan caught a glimpse of himself in the rearview and saw that he was smiling. He eased the Charger onto the gravel road, and the trees swallowed the car whole.

That was how Ivan found the house.

3

Ivan wasn't sure exactly how far they'd driven off the mountain highway, but from the time he finally decided to check the Charger's odometer to when they drove into the clearing, he'd clocked two miles. He guessed there'd been at least another mile behind them, but out here in the dark with nothing but tall trees on either side of the car, and with the tension of the night's events still overshadowing clear thinking, it was impossible to tell.

Jessica must have been thinking the same thing he was,

because right before the trees had parted to let them out, she'd said, "How have we even been driving straight for this long?"

Ivan knew what she meant. The main road they'd left behind had been all curves and elevation changes as the asphalt snaked through the rocky earth, climbing into the hills, but ever since the Charger's tires had crunched onto the gravel road, Ivan had held the wheel straight and maintained a cautious twenty-five miles per hour, the road flat and straight as a ruler.

"What am I, a fucking geologist?" Ivan said.

"That's rocks."

"What?"

"A geologist studies rocks ... I think. Jonas would know."

Ivan sighed. "Well, there's damn rocks all over out here, ain't there?"

Jessica didn't respond. Pointed out the windshield. "Look."

Ivan looked. The trees had spat them out into the front yard of an old two-story farmhouse that sat staring back at them with sleepy-eyed windows with crooked shutters. The moon was visible again now that they'd left the woods, and it hung in the sky above the house like a star topping a Christmas tree, casting a champagne glow across the land.

Ivan felt that surge of desire again, something pulling him forward, letting him know it was okay to come in and visit for a while.

This is the place, he thought. *We can lay low here as long as we need to.*

Ivan had never believed in God, but right at that moment

as he grappled with the near impossibility of finding this house right when he'd needed it, he couldn't completely shake away the idea of there being a higher power.

Looks like maybe somebody is watching out for us after all, he thought. But then he thought of Jonas, his brother's neck bursting open as the bullet ripped through skin and muscle.

"Think anyone's home?" Jessica asked.

The Charger's headlights were cutting wide cones of light across the yard, and Ivan pointed to the tall grass. "Yard ain't been mowed in forever. House looks like shit. No lights on. Didn't see no mailbox or nothing indicating an address back there anywhere." *Plus, I sorta feel like we're supposed to be here. But I sure a shit ain't saying that out loud because you'll think I've lost my fucking mind.* "No, nobody's been here for a long time. It's perfect."

Ivan drove forward along the gravel driveway and then pulled to the right, driving into the grass and swooping around toward the side of the house.

"Where are you going?" Jessica asked.

"Around back. I don't think it'll happen, but in case any looky-loos happen to come down the road, I don't want our car out front."

"You think if somebody comes all this way looking for us they won't bother to check around back?"

"You know, Jess, you and Jonas had that in common. You always fucking assume the worst. Better safe than sorry, right? Maybe you're right, but it certainly won't make it *easier* to find us if I park back here."

Jessica was quiet for a second, and as Ivan rounded the back of the house, she said, "He's dead, isn't he?"

"What?"

"You said we *had* that in common."

"Dammit, no, I was—"

"Oh, that's gorgeous!" Jessica yelled.

Ivan slammed on the brakes and the Charger skidded a couple feet in the grass. His heart pounded fast in his chest. "Jesus, Jess! What the fuck?"

"What? Oh, sorry. Hey, payback for the windows. But *look*, Ivan." She pointed out her window.

Ivan leaned down and looked out the passenger window, saw the pond, its water rippling in the metallic moonlight, giving the illusion of thousands of tiny sparklers coming to life on the water's surface. Even a soulless hard-ass like Ivan had to admit to himself it was a pretty scene.

But beauty wasn't important right now.

"Let's go," he said. He pushed open his door and stepped out into the night, the air humid and sticky, sweat instantly peppering his brow and the back of his neck. He stepped up to the back door of the house and turned the knob. It was locked, which sort of surprised him, and then he figured maybe it was just stuck. Rusted or jammed, the wood swollen. He heard Jessica open and then close her door, but he didn't look back at her. Instead, he took a step backward and then kicked the door as hard as he could with his boot. It flew open and slammed into something hard, bouncing back toward him. He used his palm to stop it from swinging closed completely and was amazed to see that the door frame hadn't broken or splintered. The door had simply popped open.

Huh ... latch must be wonky. He was sure it wouldn't be the only structural oddity they'd encounter in a house as old as this one, one that looked as though it had been neglected for at least a decade, probably two.

Ivan stepped into the house and with only the moonlight to light his way he saw he was in a kitchen. The door had slammed into an ugly old refrigerator, and a big sink basin took up half the wall to his right. He turned around and stood in the open doorway and called to Jess. "You coming?"

He had expected Jessica to be right behind him, or maybe just by the car. What he saw instead was his sister standing further out in the backyard, halfway now between the Charger and the edge of the pond with its sparkling ripples.

"Jessica!" he didn't exactly mean to shout, but he did all the same. A tingle of panic that he couldn't quite understand throwing the words from his throat.

His sister spun around and then jogged through the grass, swerving around the car and then joining him inside the old kitchen. By the time she reached him, she was out of breath.

"What were you doing?" he asked, stepping back to look at her after closing the door, which seemed to hold shut just fine, even after his kick.

Jessica laughed and shook her head. "You're going to think I'm crazy."

"Already do."

She shot him the bird.

"Seriously, Jess. What were you looking at?"

Jessica ran a hand through her hair. "I must be really fucking wigged out right now. I swear to you, Ivan, I thought I saw a girl out there, standing on that little dock."

"A girl?"

"Yep. She was naked, just standing there looking down at the water. And then she dived in. I was watching, just waiting for her to come back up to the surface, you know. She couldn't stay down there forever, right? But then you called me and I sort of snapped out of it. Started thinking straight again." She smiled and laughed. "Crazy, right?"

Ivan knew there was no girl out there. Of course there wasn't.

Stress, he thought. *We're all just stressed.*

"Hey," he said, wanting to try and put his little sister's mind at ease. "If there's a naked girl out there in trouble, I feel I'm obliged to go and offer my assistance."

Jessica laughed again and shook her head. "Obligated."

"What?"

"I think you mean you're *obligated* to go and help her."

Ivan thought of Jonas again but didn't let his face betray any emotion. He just nodded and said, "Come on, let's check this place out."

As they walked out of the kitchen and started down a short hallway leading to the front of the house, Ivan almost turned around when he thought he heard the faint sound of a splash.

4

Jessica tried a light switch in the hallway before Ivan could tell her it was pointless. Of course there would be no electricity. Even if the connection to the main grid was still intact, and the fuse box had miraculously remained functional after all these years, Ivan was sure the electric bill would be long past due by now. Jessica made no comment when she flipped the switch up and down a couple times with no result, which Ivan guessed meant she wasn't surprised either. Ivan wouldn't have let her keep the lights on anyway. Even though all signs indicated the house was well isolated and hidden from any prying eyes, he didn't want to risk lighting the place up, which he felt would be akin to sending up signal flares. Just because he hadn't seen any other houses around didn't mean there weren't actually neighbors just through the trees who would notice and come investigate.

Or call the cops.

Just like parking the Charger around back—better safe than sorry.

Ivan didn't mind the dark. In fact, he felt more at home in the dark than he ever did in the light. Nighttime was his world, his playground. Nighttime was when people like him thrived. Jessica, too, even though she didn't like to admit it quite as freely as he did. Jonas was the one of the three of them who preferred the day, loved to go out into town on warm summer days and meet people, act like he wasn't a low-life piece of shit just like the rest of the family. Some folks played along, or were just genuinely nice, giving Jonas the benefit of the doubt. But others in town ... well, they knew Jonas's last name, knew trouble followed that name almost everywhere it went. They kept their distance and pretended not to see him.

"They act like I'm a stray dog who might bite," Jonas had told Ivan one day a few months ago. "It's insulting and ... it's *embarrassing.*"

When Ivan had seen the tears forming in Jonas's eyes he'd been embarrassed too. Embarrassed to have such a pussy for a little brother. "That's the way it is for us, bro," Ivan had said. "It's about fucking time you man up and accept that shit. Hell, you're what, twenty-four now? Grow up."

Grow up, Ivan thought now. *That was the last piece of advice I ever gave him. And now he's dead.*

And it's your fault.

Ivan stopped and spun around at the end of the hallway, peering into the darkness back toward the kitchen.

"What's wrong?" Jessica said from his side. "You hear something?"

"I..." Ivan cleared his throat. Listened as the house stayed silent while it stared back at him, unprovoked. "No, I guess not." He forced a laugh. "Hell, maybe I'm a little jumpy too."

What he didn't tell his sister was that even though he had heard his own inner voice have the thought—*And it's your fault*—the words hadn't really felt like they'd come from him at all. It was like a sliver of his own consciousness had somehow gone rogue, escaped from its cage and mocked him from afar.

"Ivan?"

He turned to her, and even in the dim moonlight coming through the grimy windows, he could see the look of concern on her face.

"I'm fine," he said and then pushed past her into what had once been a living room.

"Is that couch ... green?" Jessica said, leaning closer to the oblong shape pushed up against the front wall beneath the windows.

Ivan ignored her. Seeing nothing in the room except the couch that Jessica was examining and the fireplace with a brick hearth, he turned and went back into the entryway, seeing the door beneath the stairs. He popped it open and had to squint into the darkness to see the toilet.

"Gotta piss," he called over his shoulder.

Inside the bathroom, the ceiling slanted down, following the slope of the stairs, making the space feel cave-like and claustrophobic. Ivan closed the door and pulled his key ring from the pocket of his jeans, found the little penlight attached there. He clicked the button and a thin but powerful beam of light shot out, brightening the tiny room. Ivan lifted the toilet lid and did his business, leaning his head back and staring at the strings of cobwebs hanging from the ceiling like party streamers. He finished, tucked himself back into his pants, and then out of instinct he hit the flush handle.

The *whoosh* of the water flushing was loud and strong and startled him, and he jumped backward, banging his hip on the counter, which caused dust and cobwebs to fall from the ceiling and into his face. He spat and coughed and cursed, brushing it all away and then wiping his face with his t-shirt.

"Did you fall in?" Jessica called to him.

Ivan took a breath and exhaled slowly. Called back, "No. I tripped over my dick."

"Gross."

"Hey, you asked."

Ivan laughed at his own stupid joke and turned around

to face the mirror, the beam from his penlight throwing his own shadow across the walls in the enclosed space, like Ivan was surrounded by his own demons. There were dead flies and a single dead spider pooled in the sink, an insect mass grave.

Movement in the mirror—movement that didn't match his own—caused Ivan's neck to snap upward, his eyes locking onto the scene in the glass.

The mirror did not show Ivan his own reflection or the flipped image of the toilet tank and sloping ceiling behind him. Ivan froze, transfixed, the small bathroom blurring and being pulled away until all that was left was him and the mirror. He felt stuck, like a giant set of pliers had clamped onto his skull, locking him into position, his eyes unable to shut. His breathing went funny, panic seizing him, his lungs fighting for air and his head beginning to feel light.

In the mirror, Ivan was staring straight into the barrel of a pistol being aimed at him by a young cop with red hair. Behind the cop, the convenience store shelves boasted chips and candy bars and colorful air fresheners in the shapes of different fruits. The drink coolers along the back wall were humming and well lit and their glass doors looked as though they'd recently been cleaned.

Ivan knew this convenience store. He'd been in it four times over the last couple weeks.

He also knew the cop currently aiming the gun at him.

Not me, Ivan thought. *This isn't me. This is...*

It was impossible. Ivan knew it was. But another part of him, maybe the same part of his mind that had gone rogue in

the hallway and fed him thoughts that were not his own—
And it's your fault—told him it wasn't. This *was* happening.

Ivan was seeing through his dead brother's eyes. Watching Jonas's last moments alive unfold in front of him. Forced to watch again what Ivan had planned on spending a lifetime trying to forget.

Gunfire exploded from Ivan's (Jonas's) right, and there was the sound of shattering glass, a shout from the cashier behind him. The entire convenience store seemed to jitter for a millisecond, as if the building had been just as startled as the people. But Ivan hardly had time to comprehend any of this, because the young redheaded cop's eyes had popped open wide at the first sound of gunfire, and by the time the shattering glass sound had ended, the cop had given a small yelp of surprise and hopped backward and fired two clumsy shots at Ivan (Jonas).

The bathroom rushed back into clarity with such force that Ivan took a step back, grabbing his head and groaning, feeling a quick pulse of pressure that threatened to suffocate him. But just as quickly as it had arrived, it was gone, and Ivan was able to open his eyes and his lungs were working properly again and he—

He screamed.

In the mirror, he saw himself standing in the bathroom, his shadowy demons hovering all around him, hunched over, waiting to pounce, and blood was blooming from the bullet hole high up on his chest, the left side of his neck ripped open wide enough that he could see the flaps of muscle dangling. In pure desperation to make everything stop, Ivan twisted his body and punched the mirror, sending a spiderweb of cracks spreading out over the top right corner.

The bathroom door was ripped open and Jessica was there, demanding, "What the fuck are you doing?"

Ivan jumped away from her, hitting the wall, and when he looked back to the mirror, the bullet wounds were gone.

5

"Christ, stop shining that light in my eyes." Jessica held up a hand to shield her face from Ivan's penlight, and Ivan watched as whatever she must have seen on his face changed her entire demeanor. "Ivan? What's wrong? Are you ... hurt? Why did you scream?"

His whole life, Ivan had been a talker. A motormouth con artist who always had a joke or an excuse or a scheme loaded in the chamber, ready to fire. Now, with his back against the wall in the small bathroom, his head only a couple inches from the slanted ceiling, he found that he had no words. How could he even begin to explain what had just happened?

What did *just happen? What the fuck did I just see?*

But he knew perfectly well what he'd just seen. It wasn't the *what* that was causing his concern, it was the *how* that made his head spin and his breath hitch and heart hammer.

How did I just see the last moments of Jonas's life through his eyes? Like I was watching a damn video camera strapped to his head.

Jessica took a small step forward, joining him in the tiny bathroom, the smell of cigarettes permeating the space. Seeing her face up close, feeling the warmth of her closer to him and smelling the scent of her favorite brand of cigs worked to flush away (no pun intended) the dreamlike state that seemed to have found him. Jessica's presence grounded him, took his hand and guided him on steady legs back to the shore of real life.

And Ivan quickly found the answer to the *how*. The reason he was able to see Jonas's last moments was the same reason Jessica had been able to see a naked girl diving into the pond out back.

She hadn't. And neither had Ivan really experienced what had come over him after he'd pissed in the water-stained toilet.

Stress, he thought again, the same way he'd explained away Jessica seeing her mirage by the pond. *Or fuck, maybe it's some sort of PTSD*, Ivan realized. *I mean, shit, I saw my own brother get his neck blown open. That's bound to fuck anybody up, right?*

(And it's your fault)

"Ivan?" Jessica reached out to him, and when her hand touched his arm it was as though he was jolted awake. His head clear again.

"Sorry," he said, shaking his head and pulling his arm free from her grasp. He pointed down to the sink, to the mass grave of insects. "Spider fell from the ceiling, landed on my head. Fucking thing scared the shit out of me."

Jessica looked into the sink, saw the bugs, then looked back at him. Smirked, which in the glow of the penlight looked more menacing than it should have, like she was about to tell a ghost story over a campfire. "Well, if you're going to shit yourself, at least you're already in the bathroom."

Ivan laughed, and the sound echoed through the bathroom.

"But if you don't mind, will you get the hell out of here so I can pee?" Jessica said, stepping back to let Ivan out.

When she was finished, she and Ivan headed up the stairs, bracing themselves as the steps creaked and groaned with their footfalls. Ivan kept the penlight angled down to the floor, and together they swept the hallway, finding a full bathroom and three bedrooms all of equal size. Ivan shone the light into the corner of the first bedroom and said, "Looks like somebody had a good time here at some point."

Jessica saw what looked like an empty can and bottle of something else—maybe vodka or rum, they didn't venture close enough to check—and nodded. "Think they were running too?" Jessica asked.

Ivan stepped back into the hall. "Everyone is running from something."

After finding no beds and nothing else of interest upstairs, they returned to the living room and Ivan shut off the penlight. He pointed to the couch under the front windows—and yeah, the damn thing *was* green—and said, "Go ahead and get some sleep. I'll stay up and keep watch."

"You're going to stay up all night?"

"Yes. Better safe than sorry."

Jessica sat on the couch. Yawned. "What if they find us?"

Ivan shook his head. "I don't think they will. Not here, anyway."

"But what if they do?"

Ivan lifted his t-shirt, exposing the gun tucked into the waistband of his jeans. The same gun that he'd shot the cop with outside the convenience store and had gotten Jonas killed. "You know I'm not going back," he said. "You can try and get out of here in the Charger, try your luck. But me ... I'll go down swinging if I have to."

Jessica didn't protest. She looked through the darkness and held his gaze, a shared thought between brother and sister. Then she yawned again, nodded, and lay down on the couch.

"What the...," she said, sitting back up. "There's something under..." She reached under one of the green cushions and pulled out something black and rectangular in shape. For a second, Ivan would have sworn he saw the sparkle of something gold.

"Is that a book?" he asked.

Jessica laughed. "Yeah. Feels sorta like that Bible Mama used to keep on her nightstand. You remember that old thing?"

Ivan did remember. He grunted and said, "A lot of good all that praying ever did her."

Jessica nodded. "Amen." She tossed the book on the floor and lay down again. "Just do me a favor and wake me up before you start shooting."

All was still and a quiet for a couple minutes, the stale, humid air inside the house settling all around Ivan, joining him and his thoughts.

"Ivan?" Jessica said from the couch, her voice soft, almost pleading.

"Yeah?"

"He's dead, isn't he?"

Ivan thought for a moment, looking for the right answer. Finally, he said, "It would be a miracle if he isn't."

Jessica said nothing. A few minutes later, Ivan heard her breathing change as she drifted off to sleep. She'd always been that way, ever since she was a little kid, able to fall asleep anywhere, no matter what was happening around her.

Ivan went quietly back to the kitchen and returned with one of the chairs from the breakfast table, careful not to bump into the walls in the dark, not wanting to wake Jessica. He set the chair down in front of the couch and sat, positioning himself so he could see out the window and would easily be able to notice anyone coming down the driveway.

The minutes began to tick by and Ivan stared out the window with his mind beginning to float away, replaying everything that had happened tonight, how quickly everything had gone wrong.

He also, for a terrifying second or two, found himself wondering if one day he'd end up getting Jessica killed too. If another of his big schemes would end in death.

Maybe Jonas was right after all, he thought. *Maybe we could have been better than this, if we'd tried.*

The truth was sad and sickening. It was now too late to ever find out.

And it's all your fault.

Ivan didn't so much as flinch this time when the words entered his mind, coming at him from every angle as if the very walls of the house had whispered to him. He thought again of the way his shadow had danced around him in the little bathroom under the stairs, his demons manifested and lurking.

"You're right," Ivan finally whispered back in the dark. "Everything's my fault."

6

Robbing convenience stores was child's play, the job of amateurs or those too stupid or too desperate to come up with something else. Sure, Ivan and Jessica and Jonas had robbed their fair share of fill-and-gos in their youth—the score ranging from a Snickers bar slipped into a pants pocket to a couple grand in cash—but they'd moved beyond that in their adulthood. Bigger jobs with much bigger paydays. Bigger risk, too. And with that bigger risk had come bigger punishment. They'd all spent time in juvie at one time or another, but Ivan was the only sibling who'd won the big ticket and done an actual stint in prison. Twice.

It was the boredom that had driven him mad, the bird-in-a-cage feeling when all Ivan felt he was meant to do was fly. The routine and structure were no problem, and the other inmates hadn't been much to worry about either (Ivan had always been able to hold his own in a fight, and never backed down). It was the lack of creativity, the lack of spontaneity and inspired action that made him want to shove an ice pick in his ear if only to end the mundane.

That second stint, he'd seriously considered suicide, had in fact been deep into the process of selecting the most efficient method to kill himself when he got lucky. Overcrowded and underfunded, the prison system was forced to clear out some prisoners with lesser or nearly finished sentences to make room for some bigger, badder apples. Ivan was selected, technically released for good behavior—and when Jonas came and picked him up, Ivan swore he would never tell anyone how close he'd come to ending his own life. But he did make the promise to them and to himself—letting everyone know he would die before he'd let the state lock him away again.

Now, Jonas was the one who was dead. Ivan had kept himself alive only to get his brother killed.

The job was supposed to be easy—which was probably the first sign that Ivan should have abandoned it. Even he was smart enough to understand the validity of the old adage *If it sounds too good to be true, it is.* But money was getting low, and no other promising opportunities seemed to be on the horizon for any of the three siblings, so Ivan eventually convinced himself and his brother and sister that this job was perfect for them. Would give them some breathing room—maybe even that new start Jonas was always talking about.

Ivan had learned through the criminal grapevine that a small convenience store nearly two hours from their hometown was being used as a drop location for the Abatelli crime syndicate, which was essentially the Virginia mob. Ivan had heard stories of the Abatellis' brutality—particularly that of one of the leaders, Francis Abatelli, who rumor had it had once locked a man's skull in a vise grip and tightened it until the man's brain oozed through his eyes. But, after thinking about it, Ivan figured the little convenience store score would be chump change in the vast Abatelli empire, and that an operation of their size probably budgeted for the occasional hit. Plus, Ivan's plan did not include him and his siblings sitting around and waiting to find out if they'd poked the bear. Ivan had already planned on driving south, probably to Florida, just like he'd told Jessica, long before the nightmare had unfolded at the convenience store with the cops. He'd been desperate to get away from home, feeling the well of luck running dry there, and he was afraid that if he'd told Jonas and Jessica he was planning on fleeing the state permanently after they pulled the convenience store job, they wouldn't have agreed.

There was supposed to be a cash pickup that night. Word on the street was it happened the third Tuesday of every month. At exactly eleven o'clock, a black SUV would pull up to the store, a man would get out of the back seat and walk inside, and the cashier would hand over a case of beer from behind the counter. The cardboard box, sporting the logo and imagery of a different brand of beer each month, was of course not full of aluminum cans but tightly wrapped stacks of cash. The street guessed that the value of that case of beer usually ranged anywhere from fifty grand to upwards of a few hundred thousand.

Ivan couldn't get a clear answer on where the money came from. Some guys thought it came from the usual, drugs and weapons; others thought it was fees paid to Abatelli hitmen for jobs well done. Ivan didn't much care where the money came from, because what he did know was that it was dirty. And dirty money was easily up for grabs.

He explained the situation to Jessica and Jonas, told them once they had that box of cash they'd all be free for a while.

Money like that would go a long way. Jonas had been the one to ask the question that Ivan knew was coming, the one he couldn't quite shake himself.

"If it's so easy, and everybody knows this is happening every month, why hasn't anybody else tried to steal it?"

The answer Ivan had used to convince himself and his siblings was this: "They're all too chickenshit to risk ruffling the Abatelli feathers."

"And we aren't?" Jonas asked.

Ivan smiled. Pointed at his brother. "See, that's exactly what I mean. Those mob goons' reputation is playing phantom bodyguard to their money. They can't be everywhere at once, so they have to use all those boogeyman stories about payback and punishment to scare everyone away from taking shots at them. They know they're going to get hit now and again. Nothing they can do about it. So let's be one of those hits, what d'ya say?"

Jonas had stayed quiet.

"Jess?" Ivan looked to his sister.

Jessica shrugged. "Hell, I'm in. That's a lot of dough."

Outvoted as usual, Jonas agreed. Probably thinking if he came along he could be the voice of reason if needed.

Ivan was glad Jonas had agreed, because Jonas was the one who was going to go inside and get the box. Ivan had already made the trip out to the convenience store a few times in the week leading up to the hit, cursing at all the damn gas money he'd pumped into the Charger, but remembering that the payday was going to do much more than just reimburse him. He'd gone inside and checked the place out, bought some snacks and drinks, made small talk with the cashier who worked the night shifts—a guy probably about Ivan's age with buzzed hair and a small scar over his left eyebrow, the tattoo of a Teenage Mutant Ninja Turtle on his forearm—who was pleasant enough and didn't seem to suspect anything about Ivan's presence. Each visit, Ivan did his best to lean and look over the counter in hopes of spying a case of beer on the floor, but of course there wasn't one. No present under the tree until the night Santa's elf arrived.

The store itself sat right off the lonely two-lane highway that led into the mountains, and as Ivan sat parked in the lot eating whatever junk food and soda he'd purchased, the number of cars that passed by on the road in the thirty or so minutes he stayed never hit double digits. The odds of witnesses were going to be slim.

Ivan knew Jonas would need to be the one to go inside because Jonas was the most unassuming looking, had a baby face that always cried innocence. On the night of the pickup, Ivan knew that the cashier would be on alert and had probably been instructed by the Abatellis to shoot first and ask questions later. Ivan would swear that he wasn't willingly setting Jonas up to be sacrificed but truly believed his brother had the best temperament for the execution of the job.

Plus, if the cashier had any brains whatsoever and saw Ivan, who had only just recently begun frequenting the store, arrive on the same night as the pickup, all those warning bells about himself that Ivan had worked to avoid in the cashier's mind might suddenly begin to go off as the man worked backwards and put together the puzzle pieces.

Jessica was too giddy sometimes, and prone to erratic

behavior. Ivan had once seen her kick off a minivan's side-view mirror and then slash two of its tires because the owner had parked so close to the Charger that Jessica could barely open her door to get in. The driver, your typical suburban soccer mom, had actually been in the driver's seat and had watched this all happen with a look of shock and fear, repeatedly hitting the door lock button as if the lock would somehow grow stronger with each click. When Jessica was finished, she'd spat onto the driver's window, flipped the woman the bird, and then squeezed herself into the Charger and Ivan had driven off.

It had to be Jonas who went into the store.

7

It might have been unlucky timing—hell, Ivan and his siblings knew all about bad luck, were practically experts—or maybe the guy with the Ninja Turtle tattoo behind the counter had had some sort of silent alarm button on the floor, something he could activate without attempted robbers noticing, and the two cops who'd shown up had just happened to be right down the road during their normal patrol route.

But, in his heart, what Ivan suspected had really happened all went back to what Jonas had asked on that day Ivan had told them about the job. The same question that had bothered Ivan in the beginning as well, the one he'd talked himself out of, making himself believe a false narrative because his greed and impatience had taken over.

"If it's so easy, and everybody knows this is happening every month, why hasn't anybody else tried to steal it?"

It had been a setup, a trap, a test—any of those fit the *real* narrative. The one that Ivan had blinded himself from. That was why the information about the convenience store drop site seemed to be flowing so freely along the chatter lines. That was why, if this monthly rendezvous had in fact been occurring for who knew how long, nobody had attempted to steal the cash from under the Abatellis' noses. People stayed away because the whole thing felt fishy—*too fucking good to be true*.

Looking back on it now, it made sense that that police might have caught wind of the scheduled drop too, or, Ivan figured, there was also a strong possibility the cops who'd shown up were on the Abatelli payroll. There to snuff out any potential trouble, set fire and send a message to would-be transgressors of the Abatelli empire.

There to create another story to add to the reputation. To scare away folks just like Ivan and Jessica and Jonas. Not all the bodyguards, it turned out, were phantoms.

They'd blasted music for most of the trip, but Ivan snapped off the radio once they were about fifteen minutes away, and by the time he drove the Charger into the store's parking lot at just before ten p.m., the three siblings had fallen into the familiar silence of those who were mentally preparing for the task at hand. Ivan pulled the car alongside one of the gas pump islands, allowing the pumps to act as a sort of barrier between them and the storefront. Ivan killed the headlights but left the engine running. Jessica got out of the car and started acting like she was about to start pumping gas, fiddling with the buttons and lifting the nozzle. Ivan looked into the backseat and saw Jonas tucking his pistol into his pants, his long baggy t-shirt easily concealing it.

"Loaded?" Ivan asked.

Jonas nodded. "Yeah, but you know I'm not going to shoot him."

Ivan nodded back. "You won't have to. But it's always nice to have one or two to fire off to scare a motherfucker."

Jonas leaned to the side to catch a glimpse of the guy behind the counter through the big glass windows, then he closed his eyes and took a deep breath, letting it out in a tired sigh. When he opened his eyes again he looked at Ivan and said, "This is it, right? We get this cash and we're done."

Ivan knew this wasn't the time to argue with his brother. This conversation should have happened during the two-hour drive and now it was too late. He would say whatever he needed to for Jonas to get the fuck out of the car and get the box of money, but he found that when he spoke his next words, he actually meant them. "You'll get your share and then you can do whatever you want, Joe. You can start a business or go blow it on hookers and meth for all I care. Jess and I'll be fine."

Jonas cracked a small smile. "I'll leave the hookers for you."

He pulled the handle and popped open the door, standing from the car and making a dramatic show of stretching his back—using the movement to scan the parking lot, checking for any signs of witnesses. Ivan had been here enough times at this time of night to know that they'd be able to see approaching headlights from either direction in plenty of time to get out of there before an innocent bystander could interrupt.

Jonas walked across the parking lot toward the store, calling over his shoulder to Jess, "You want a Snickers?"

"Sure," Jessica called back. "And a Cherry Coke."

Jonas gave a thumbs-up and strolled casually into the store.

Ivan gripped the wheel with both hands and leaned forward, watching Jonas walk through the aisles, pretending to browse. His brother pulled open one of the cooler doors and grabbed a Cherry Coke, then headed for the counter.

Jonas made the move. He set the Coke on the counter and in the same motion reached behind his back and pulled the pistol free from his waistband. He whipped it forward and aimed it at the cashier's head. The guy with the Ninja Turtle took a quick step back and held up his hands. Ivan saw Jonas's mouth moving but couldn't make out what he was saying. But he did see the cashier shake his head, his eyes narrowed and angry. Jonas thrust the gun forward, pointed to the floor behind the counter and—

And that was when Ivan was distracted by movement in the rearview. His body flinched and his eyes darted up to the mirror and like an apparition that had silently conjured itself out of thin air, he was shocked to see a police cruiser parked perpendicularly behind the gas pumps with its lights off. He'd never heard the sound of the engine over the rumbling of the Charger's.

Motherfuckers, Ivan thought. *They rolled in with no lights ...*

but how? They couldn't have been on the highway like that, they would have...

They were waiting. Shit, *the bastards were parked and waiting, probably right across the road in the field and we never fucking saw them. It's too damn dark out here.*

Ivan then remembered Jessica, wondered why she hadn't warned him. He spun around and looked toward the rear passenger side of the car, and he saw why. There was a cop with his gun drawn and aimed at Jess, motioning for her to step toward the front of the car. Jessica had her hands up and was saying something Ivan couldn't hear. Ivan looked away and back toward the front of the store, saw another cop. He was short and broad, with red hair that seemed to glow crimson in the harsh fluorescents. He had his pistol drawn too, and he was half-crouched down as he eased the store's door open.

Ivan saw Jonas spin around, probably alerted by a bell or some electronic chime that went off when the cop opened the door. Jonas's trained his gun toward the door, and Ivan saw the flash of dismay light up Jonas's face when he realized a police officer had just entered the mix.

"I said hands up, and step out slowly!" A voice pulled Ivan away from the scene inside the store. He glanced to the front of the car, where Jessica was bent over with her hands on the hood, and the cop had his gun pointed in Ivan's direction. "Now!"

I'll die before I go back, Ivan's brain screamed. *I'll fucking die.*

He raised his hands off the steering wheel and held them up for the cop to see, then he looked back to the front of the store, saw the cop inside had reached the counter, was standing only a few feet in front of Jonas. The two men had their guns pointed at each other, but even from the distance of the Charger Ivan could see Jonas's resolve faltering. He had to do something, but the options were severely limited.

If we go down, Ivan thought, *we're going to go down shooting.*

Jessica must have read his mind, because when Ivan looked over the hood and into his sister's eyes, she shook her head ever so slightly. *No.*

Goddammit, I'm the only one with any balls around here.

Ivan slowly reached a hand down for the handle and pulled, stepping out of the car gingerly. The cop was screaming for him to slow down, even though Ivan didn't think it was possible for him to move any slower. *He's jumpy*, Ivan thought.

"Hands on the hood!" the cop yelled.

Ivan put his hands on the hood, moving as close to the front of the car as he could.

"Don't fucking move!" The cop had the gun wavering between Jessica and Ivan, and the look on his face told Ivan the guy wasn't quite sure what to do now that he had both of them in front of him. He was outnumbered, gun or no gun.

Ivan looked at Jessica but found that his sister was apparently no longer interested in him or his plans. Instead, with her hands still on the hood, Jessica had twisted her neck around and was doing her best to watch the showdown between Jonas and the cop inside the store.

"He'll be alright," Ivan said.

Jessica didn't move, didn't speak.

Then the moment that would become both the miracle and the curse happened. One of the HVAC units on the convenience store's roof rumbled to life in a quick burst of air and vibrating metal. The sound was like an eruption in the night, and the cop who'd had his gun hovering between Jessica and Ivan jumped back and spun around toward the noise, gun raised. His back was to Ivan for only half a second, but that was all it took. Ivan, with speed even he was surprised he possessed, pulled his right hand off the hood of the Charger and reached behind him, grabbing his pistol and then quickly bringing it around and firing off two rounds. The first one hit the cop in the back of his head with a sound like somebody taking a hammer to a melon, and the second bullet sailed past everything and found the front of the store, shattering the window next to the cashier.

And that was when the cop inside the store fired his shots.

Years of street smarts and gut instinct reaction took hold of both Jessica and Ivan, and without question or hesitation, both of them had jumped back into the car. Without thinking, only knowing he needed his hands free for the steering wheel and to shift the car into gear, Ivan tossed the gun into the back of the car, where it clattered to the floorboard. The tires squealed on the asphalt and then they were gone, a blur down the pitch black highway, the gun chittering and chattering across the floorboard as Ivan took a curve too fast, making him think, *Dear God, just don't let it go off.*

But all this wasn't before Ivan had glimpsed the cop's bullets tear into his only brother, and the realization that this entire night had been doomed from the start had begun to sink in.

I'm such a fucking idiot, he thought.

They had no money, and now Jonas was dead.

And it's all your fault.

8

The sun had risen, bright streaks of light poking holes through a blanket of storm clouds on the horizon. The tall trees surrounding the house swayed back and forth in the wind. Ivan blinked several times, the world in front of him coming back into focus, the memory of what had happened last night washed away and replaced with a sense of disorientation. He was still seated in the chair from the breakfast table, his neck and back stiff. His eyes dry and burning. He blinked several more times, trying to flush away the burn, and as a ray of sunshine slipped through a gap in the clouds and lit a streak across the yard, only a one-word question repeated itself in his head.

How?

How was this possible?

His last waking memory had been of getting the kitchen chair and sitting down in front of the couch while Jessica had drifted off to sleep. He'd been staring out the window into the darkness, the moon's iridescence acting as a gentle nightlight. He did the math in his head, tried to guess what time that had been, when the two of them had finally settled in for the night in this abandoned old house that had been their saving grace. Figured that even if it had taken much longer than he had assumed between them flying out of the convenience store parking lot and then finding the house, the shortest period of time he could have been sitting in the chair by the window was four or five hours.

It had felt like nothing more than a blink of the eye. A blackout of all time and space while his mind had relived those awful moments where Jonas had been killed and Ivan and Jessica had fled.

Impossible.

He supposed he could have fallen asleep sitting up, but he didn't *feel* like he'd been asleep. In fact, now, rubbing his eyes with his knuckles and standing from the chair, his knees creaking and his lower back on fire, Ivan felt more exhausted than he'd felt in a long time, the evening's adrenaline and

Stress ... stress is fucking with your head, man.

stress burning away his energy, depleting his reserves.

Though it was unlikely, left with no other plausible explanation, Ivan eventually resigned himself to believing that he had somehow managed to fall asleep shortly after Jessica, and his dreams of the nightmare at the convenience store had kept him company all the way to morning. His body shutting down in a failed attempt to recharge.

The soft sounds of Jessica's snores—more the purr of a kitten, really—caused Ivan to look away from the window and down to his sister. She had rolled over onto her side, facing the back of the green couch, her legs pulled up toward her chest. The back of her shirt had pulled up, and Ivan saw the polka-dot scars there from the time their father had used Jessica as an ashtray. The sight of these scars usually brought with them a flood of memories creating waves of anger in

Ivan, but—and maybe it was the exhaustion refusing to loosen its grip—this morning he found that they only brought with them a deep sense of sadness.

A low pair, he thought. *The deck's always been stacked against us. The house always wins.*

Jonas's voice filled Ivan's thoughts. *You let it win, Ivan. You never even bothered to try switching tables or playing a different game.*

Ivan spun around, his knee knocking the chair sideways with a startling scrape of its feet on the warped wooden floor. It had felt as if Jonas had spoken from just over Ivan's shoulder, whispering in his ear. The room was empty, and when a gust of wind blew across the yard, air whistled from the fireplace and Ivan saw a dusting of ashes dance across the hearth. He looked back to Jessica to see if the noise he'd made with the chair had woken her, but she remained unmoving, her soft purring still singing its song. She was a heavy sleeper. Hell, they all were. Had to learn to be, because otherwise they'd never have gotten any sleep as children—too many screaming matches, too many loud televisions and drunken commentary, too many fists through walls and beer bottles shattered.

When your waking hours were a nightmare, you learned to stay in your dreams.

Ivan shook his head, scattering away another rush of childhood memories the same way the ash had scattered across the hearth. He had to piss and was nearly to the door to the bathroom beneath the stairs when the smell of coffee and cooked bacon hit him. Ivan froze in the gray morning light, and as if a bottle had been uncorked somewhere, sounds from the kitchen rushed at him from down the short hallway and around the front of the stairs: sizzling meat in a pan, the *clink-clink* of a stirring spoon, a cabinet door opening and closing.

And then a voice.

A voice that Ivan had known he'd never hear again except in his nightmares.

Jonas called from the kitchen, "Are you going to eat, or are you going to fucking stand there?"

9

Just like Ivan knew it was impossible that he had merely blinked and found himself suddenly watching the sunrise after he'd sat in the chair to take on the night watch while Jessica slept, he also knew it was impossible that the words he had just heard come from the kitchen and greet him in the home's entryway had been spoken by Jonas.

Jonas was dead. Ivan would never be able to erase the horrible image of the bullets knocking his brother back, tearing the flesh of his neck. There was no way Jonas had survived that.

But...

But what if he had? What if the cop's shots hadn't been fatal after all?

Didn't change anything. Even if Jonas had managed to survive his injuries, he sure as shit wouldn't be here now. He'd be laid up in a hospital bed right now, probably hooked up to all sorts of tubes and monitors, and definitely handcuffed to the bed's railing.

And how would he even find us? Ivan wondered, still holding on to the tiny sliver of fantasy that his brother had lived to fight another day. None of the three of them ever used smartphones, opting for the cheaper pay-as-you-go flip phones you could grab at the gas station, a criminal's best friend, so Jonas wouldn't have been able to use any of those fancy tracking apps you always saw people using on TV, the ones that parents used to stalk their children. And even though there were several times throughout their lives that had caused Ivan to believe that a sort of sibling-sixth-sense connected him and Jessica and Jonas, Ivan doubted it was strong enough to use as a GPS tracking beacon.

Stop it, Ivan scolded himself. *Jonas is dead.*

He took a step around the front of the stairs. *Okay, motherfucker, then who's in the kitchen?*

It was a good question. The aroma of coffee and bacon was growing stronger, and Ivan figured that if whoever was waiting for him down the hall had meant them any harm, they probably wouldn't have cooked for them like Ivan and Jessica were guests at the world's shittiest bed-and-breakfast.

His voice... Ivan took another step and then stopped. Regardless of Ivan's lack of understanding of what possible scenario in the Universe's vast superhighway of outcomes might have allowed his younger brother to end up in the house this morning, the one thing that Ivan was certain of was that the voice that had greeted him belonged to Jonas. He would have bet his life on it.

And this wasn't like in the living room, Ivan thought,

starting to walk again. *When I heard him then it was different, like he was a ... ghost. A voice in the shadows.*

Ivan reached the kitchen entryway and stopped, suddenly overcome with emotion that silenced all his parsing of logic. He slipped into a warm bath of love, his heart swelling and rejoicing at the sight before him. And then, Ivan laughed, thinking again of his mother's worn and scuffed Bible that had always lived on her nightstand, and the way she had always greeted them on the Easter mornings of their youth.

"*Good morning, children! He is risen!*"

He is risen, Ivan thought. *That motherfucker has risen.*

"Jonas?" Ivan's voice creaked. "Joe?"

The unmistakable image of Jonas stood at the stove, his back to Ivan. He wore the same cargo pants and gray t-shirt he'd worn last night. Ivan's eyes looked to the top of his kid brother's head, saw the tuft of black hair sticking up just next to his crown, a cowlick that Jonas had had since he was a tyke. Something about that tuft of black hair standing on end sealed the deal for Ivan. He didn't know how, and he didn't *care* how, but the person standing in front of the stove was Jonas. His brother. The brother Ivan thought he'd gotten killed.

The world seemed to grow brighter, a pressing weight that had been slowly settling onto Ivan's chest and shoulders, subtly suffocating him, sprouted wings and took flight, making Ivan feel as if he was floating, that if there hadn't been a ceiling over his head he would soon find himself snatched up by the breeze and carried over the treetops like a child's lost balloon.

At the stove, Jonas turned his head just enough for Ivan to make out the tip of his brother's nose and asked, "Scrambled or over easy?"

Ivan surveyed the counter and saw a carton of eggs, the empty packet of bacon, a loaf of Wonder Bread (a staple of their childhood), and further down near the other side, a large can of instant coffee that must have been some knockoff brand because Ivan had never seen it before. There was a teakettle meant to look like a rooster next to the coffee can, along with a tin mug that looked like what Ivan's father used to use out by the firepit in the backyard.

"Dad's coffee was never just coffee, remember?" Jonas said from the stove, as if he'd been able to read Ivan's thoughts, giving credence to that notion of a sibling sixth sense. His head was turned down toward the pan on the burner, tendrils of steam rising and parting around his face. "He always said he needed a little flavor."

Ivan found himself nodding, unable to look away from the tin mug. "That was my first taste of whiskey," he said. "Probably was for all of us."

"How old were you, six, seven?"

"Something like that."

"I was ten."

Ivan nodded again. "You fought it off as long as you could. I remember."

"Yep."

"I guess you always knew better. Even back then you were the smart one."

Jonas worked a wooden spatula across the pan, stirring

the eggs. "A lot of good it did me. You're getting scrambled, by the way. Since you never fucking answered."

Ivan pulled his stare away from the tin mug on the counter and looked over to Jonas. Found that he was hit with a sudden urge to rush to his little brother and throw his arms around him, wanted to apologize profusely—not just for last night, for getting Jonas shot, but for everything: a lifetime of ignorance and misguidance and for never letting Jonas try to live the life he dreamed of. For being so selfish and angry about his own lack of accomplishment and status in life that he was determined to drag anyone around him down too.

Because you're nothing, Ivan's own voice whispered to him in his head. *You're less than nothing. Loser. Wannabe. Poser ... you consider yourself a criminal and you're not even very good at being that either. I mean, look at last night. All the signs were there ... you should have known!*

Last night...

The convenience store scene fast-forwarded through Ivan's mind again, no details changed or altered, ending where it always did—the image of Jonas jerking backward as the bullets struck. Ivan and Jessica making their escape.

"Jonas ... how did you—"

"Take a seat," Jonas said. He reached out and grabbed a couple slices of Wonder Bread from the bag and tossed it into the pan with the eggs. "Food's almost ready. And wait till you try this coffee. Bro, it's unlike anything I've ever tasted."

Maybe it was the grumbling from his stomach that pushed away Ivan's question, or maybe it was simply because, despite everything else, in that moment Ivan wanted—*needed*—to believe that Jonas was alive more than anything he'd ever wanted or needed before.

Because if his little brother really had survived the shooting at the convenience store, maybe Ivan would be able to live the rest of his life without that suffocating guilt crushing him until it ground him down to nothing but a fine powder of bone.

He moved around to the far side of the square breakfast table, moving past the empty spot where the chair he'd taken last night was missing, and began to sit.

That was when he saw his gun.

10

Ivan's attention snapped to the dull black finish of his gun on the table just as he started to sit, and the sight of it was so jarring he temporarily lost his focus and nearly missed the seat, landing half-on/half-off the chair and having to grab the table to keep from falling over.

"You okay there, bro? What are ya, hungover?" Jonas asked from the stove.

Ivan didn't say anything. Stared at the gun on the table and found that the sight of it stirred sour emotions in his gut. Once a staple of his trade (*Trade? Who are you fucking kidding?*), a part of his lifestyle that he carried everywhere the same way a man might carry a wallet and set of keys, now the gun seemed to do nothing more than serve as a stark reminder of all the mistakes he had made, a totem of despair and shame. It pulled forward memories Ivan found he now wanted to forever forget, a lifetime of misery culminating in last night's missteps when Jonas had been—

But he's right here! He's not dead!

—killed all because Ivan had grown impatient and unable to accept his own failures.

"Ivan?"

Ivan jerked his head up from the table, found Jonas standing on the other side of it, a plate of food in one hand and the tin mug full of steaming coffee in the other. Ivan, seeing his brother's face for the first time since entering the kitchen, seeing Jonas's neck intact and without so much as a bruise or scrape or blemish, finding no crimson bloom of blood on the upper part of Jonas's chest, laughed. It was a deep, genuine laugh that seemed to boil in his core and erupt like lava, uncontrollable. The sound reverberated through the kitchen and traveled down the hallway, where it swooped in a U-turn in the entryway and returned to them like a chorus of ghosts joining in on the joke.

Ivan felt delirious.

He felt fucking wonderful. Best day of his goddamn life.

Jonas smiled a sly grin and slid the plate of food and coffee mug across the table toward him, then sat down in the chair opposite Ivan.

Ivan found he was ravenous and picked up a piece of toast, folded it like a taco shell, and then used it to scoop up some of the scrambled egg. He took a big bite and chewed. With his mouth still full, he nodded to the gun and asked, "How'd that get there? Did you grab it from the Charger?"

Jonas crossed his arms and leaned back in the chair.

"What are you talking about? It was right there when I got here. You must have put it there."

Ivan shook his head, remembering the sound the gun had made as it skedaddled across the Charger's back floorboard as he'd driven away from the gas station. Then he stopped chewing and locked eyes with his brother, seeing if maybe Jonas was messing with him. But Jonas only stared back, his face unflinching. Ivan shook his head. "I don't think so. I tossed it into the car after—"

He stopped talking, and his thoughts came to a screeching halt like they'd crashed into a brick wall. He couldn't seem to remember exactly what had happened last night. The once-prominent memories were now blurred into a tangled mess of abstract images. He remembered something about a gas station, and the Ninja Turtles. And ... the gun. Something about his gun. No ... not his, a cop's gun. Two of them. Two cops, two guns. No ... maybe three guns. And beer?

Was Jessica there? Did somebody get hurt?

Where was he now? Whose house was this?

"Have you tried the coffee yet? I'm telling you, man, it's unreal." Jonas said.

His brother's voice cleared away the fog in Ivan's mind. He snapped back to the moment, and again, the sight of Jonas sitting across from him filled him with unexpected relief and happiness.

Ivan grinned and reached for the mug. "You didn't put any whiskey in it, right?"

Jonas shook his head. "Dad drank it all."

Ivan raised the mug. "Cheers."

He took a sip, and when the liquid splashed across his tongue and down his throat, Ivan realized Jonas had been correct. He didn't know this brand of coffee, but it was the tastiest, richest flavor he'd ever experienced. He took another sip and then, unable to help himself, Ivan began to gulp the coffee, overcome with an unquenchable thirst. The coffee was too hot, and it burned his throat, but he didn't care. He felt the tears streaming from his eyes as he finished off the last drop and then set the mug back on the table, burping, and then laughing.

But the laugh instantly turned into a scream.

Jonas was leaning forward, his hands flat on the table, hunched over with his shoulders pushed up to his ears. He looked like an animal ready to pounce. His eyes were solid black orbs, piercingly dark and empty, the skin around them sagging and peeling away as if melting. Black, poisoned veins sprawled across his forehead and cheeks, like he'd been injected with ink. A soft wheezing sound caught Ivan's attention, and he looked down and saw the bullet hole in the upper part of Jonas's chest, the blood and pus congealing into a grotesque snot-yellow and green and dark red while black blood bubbled from the wound as the thing that had been Jonas struggled to breathe.

The blurred and tangled mess that had become of last night's events suddenly straightened and cleared in Ivan's mind, and the guilt crashed down on him in a tidal wave of force. His own breath caught in his chest and his heart did a funny flutter and Ivan felt a panic attack begin to overcome him, blacken his vision. He coughed and pushed back from the table, standing and bumping it with is hip.

You did this, his own voice said to him, clawing through the chaos in his head, making sure to be heard. *You killed him. And now look what he's become.*

"I'm sorry!" Ivan yelled, his back against the kitchen wall. "I didn't mean it! I thought I could make things better for us! It was supposed to be the last job!" He ran through all the excuses, not even sure anymore which were true and which were lies. "I'm sorry, Joe!"

The thing that had once been Ivan's brother pushed itself up from the table with clumsy, twitching jerks, bones and tendons cracking and snapping. Ivan pushed against the wall with all his strength, hoping he might simply pass through it like a phantom, freeing himself from this nightmare. Piss trickled down his leg, but he never even had a second to consider his own embarrassment because the thing that had once been Jonas turned his head to the right, bringing front and center the gaping hole in its neck. The shredded muscles and inside of the flaps of skin were lined with yellowed teeth, sharp and crowded, and a small black tongue rolled around inside the wound, flopping like a fish washed up on the shore.

A mouth. Sweet Christ, it's a fucking mouth!

"*Your ... fault...*" Jonas's voice came out of the neck-mouth in a breathy rush of air, afflicted with pain and suffering, sounding both far away and right inside Ivan's head at the same time. The teeth-lined flaps of skin chomped out of rhythm with the words, and the black tongue *clucked* twice.

The sound of the clucking tongue pulled something free from the whirlwind of panic in Ivan's mind, making him think of a chicken, and he remembered the run-down chicken coop he'd seen last night when he'd pulled the Charger around the back of the house.

Outside, he thought, struggling to think straight. *I've got to get the hell out of this house.*

The thing that had once been Jonas jerked its head back around, black eyes landing on Ivan like macabre spotlights. The movement collided with Ivan's thought and jumpstarted him back into action. His instincts took over again, the way they always had on the streets, and he lunged forward and snatched his gun from the table. Raised the weapon and leveled it at Jonas's chest. Which caused Ivan's eyes to drift to the oozing bullet wound that already existed there, and just as he was thinking, *Can I even kill him? Can I kill him again?*, a new voice shouted from Ivan's left.

"What the hell are you doing?"

Ivan spun toward the voice, keeping his gun raised, and found a cop standing just out of the hallway. A cop he recognized instantly as the one who'd been in the convenience store parking lot and had ordered Ivan from the car. There was a quarter-sized black dot of a bullet hole just above the cop's right eye, and the eyeball looked like a deflated sac, green mucus tears falling down the man's cheeks. The cop had his hand out, holding his own black pistol, pointing it at Ivan.

Ivan didn't hesitate. He fired three shots into the cop's chest. But as he was in the middle of squeezing the trigger, as the bullets flew from the barrel and across the kitchen, striking their target with sick, meaty thuds, the air in the room seemed to shift, Ivan's vision blurring and buzzing, and through that blur, the cop's image changed, as if somebody were shaking him, sifting away the debris to reveal the truth.

Ivan saw Jessica's face appear, her eyes wide, her mouth frozen in an O shape as the bullets knocked her back. Ivan heard her give off one surprised gasp, and then she fell sideways, striking her head on the wall with a crunch before crumpling into a lifeless heap on the floor.

11

Just as the night sky had switched to morning sun in the blink of Ivan's eye, an unmeasured, unnoticed passing of time, the kitchen blinked itself back to being still and silent and empty. The air lost the aroma of bacon and eggs and coffee, and when Ivan surveyed the dingy space he saw the counters bare, the stove undisturbed. No food, no pans, no mess. He glanced down to the table and found nothing atop it. No plate, no coffee mug. No crumbs. Just a thin layer of dust, partially disturbed where the gun had lain.

The gun.

Ivan looked down to his hand, which was still clutching his pistol. Let the piece fall and clatter onto the table, smearing more dust across the scarred wood. The noise seemed deafening, and Ivan winced. His blood was rushing in his ears, ocean waves crashing, and as he pressed himself back against the wall and put his hands on his head and tried to breathe normally, tried to fight away the shock that wanted to dominate his body, only then did he realize what other great change the kitchen had endured.

Jonas, or the thing that had looked like Jonas, was gone.

Ivan slapped himself across the face, trying to wake from what was surely a nightmare, but when he looked from the corner of his eye and saw what he knew was the shape of his dead sister lying on the floor, he knew it was a nightmare he would never wake from.

He turned his head and looked. Jessica was lying on her side, facing him, her legs pulled up toward her chest, nearly identical to the way she'd been lying on the ugly green couch.

Asleep, Ivan thought. *She's still asleep.*

But Jessica's eyes were not closed. They were wide open, staring nowhere and everywhere at once, and Ivan knew no matter where he moved throughout the kitchen those eyes would always follow him.

A coldness did not so much seep into his blood as flood him. Icy detachment that felt more robotic than anything human. Preprogrammed and autonomous. Looking at his dead sister, Ivan felt whatever was left of his soul die inside him, leaving behind nothing but a husk that would soon wither away.

All your fault.

The words were comprised of not just Ivan's voice but the echoes of Jonas's and Jessica's too. The three voices came together in a sorrowful harmony. Haunting and perhaps a tad beautiful.

It was true. It was his fault.

I killed the only people I ever loved ... the only people who ever loved me.

Ivan felt his feet moving with no recollection of telling them to, and his right hand shot out and scooped up his gun, tucking it into his waistband the way he'd done a thousand times before. He walked and stood over Jessica's body, doing his best to avoid her death stare. Off to the side, a black shape caught his eye, and he remembered the way the cop had been holding a black pistol in his hand. Now, crouching down and getting a better look, Ivan saw that what had really been in Jessica's hand was the worn black book she'd found under the couch cushion.

Ivan stared at the book for a long time, not touching it, waiting for the kitchen to stop playing one of its tricks. But the book did not change.

Etched into the front cover in gold lettering was his own name.

IVAN

He found he wanted to pick the book up, flip through its pages and find out how his story was going to end.

You already know. That chorus of voices again.

Ivan nodded and stood. He did know. Only one option left.

Should have done it a long time ago, he thought.

Mercifully, the voices did not respond.

12

After carrying Jessica's body outside and across the yard and dumping her into the pond, Ivan sat down on the end of the dock with his back to the water, facing the old house, the Charger still parked by the back door. The sun had burned the clouds away, and it glinted off the car's chrome, making Ivan squint.

It all happened so fast, he thought. Not just the last twenty-four hours, the moments that would lead him here to this dock, but his entire life.

He'd blinked, and it was gone.

Do it.

This time the voice in his head was his father's, and as Ivan put the pistol in his mouth and pulled the trigger, he caught a faint whiff of coffee and whiskey.

A splash, and then nothing.

DECLAN
II

1

Declan turned the page of the book and found the next one blank, reaching the end of the story about the man named Ivan and his brother and sister. He didn't so much stop reading as he did come up for air, because Declan felt like he'd been holding his breath for the last few pages, reading the tiny, crammed-tight words as fast as his brain would allow.

"What a fun little story," Declan said, his voice loud in the quiet kitchen. He flipped through the rest of the book's pages, looking for some indication of who the author had been or who might have published it, but the remaining pages were all blank, as was the back cover. Declan flipped back to the beginning of the book and closed it and then crinkled his brow. Flipped the book over again, and then back once more to the front.

Both sides were now blank. The gold letters spelling out

the name IVAN had left behind no trace. Declan's confusion was only stemmed because right then something outside the back door's window caught his eye. Something long and black and...

Declan jumped up from his seat, dropping the book on the table where it landed open and facedown, as if Declan were trying to keep his place in the text.

A car, Declan realized. *Somebody's here.* And then there was an uneasy quiver in his heart. Because the front half of the car was completely visible through the glass pane, and Declan, not even much of a car guy, was still able to piece together the make and model from the distinctive body style.

It was a black Dodge Charger.

Under normal circumstances, Declan should have felt fear, anxiousness, or at least some apprehension. But in that moment, his mind still half-living within the pages of the strange book he'd found, Declan found himself more driven by curiosity and ... yes, he had to admit, excitement. Whoever had written the story about Ivan had obviously used this house as their setting and inspiration, which meant they had to have been here before. All artists pulled from real life for their work, so maybe the person who had written the story actually drove a black Dodge Charger. Maybe the author was the home's previous owner and had stopped by to say hello. How perfect that the house would change hands from one writer to another.

Declan was smiling when he reached the back door and pulled it open.

But the smile vanished the moment the cool morning air hit his face and the backyard came into clear view.

The Charger was gone.

2

A man's laughter echoed through the yard, and Declan felt an icy finger of fear run down his spine until he realized the laughter was coming from him. The laughter trickled off into a quiet chuckle, and Declan shook his head. Wished he really could meet the author of the Ivan story because the writer's words had been so effective that Declan had started to feel like he was actually living in the tale.

But Declan knew it wasn't just the writer's story, it was his own mindset. He still felt exhausted, even more so than before, despite the two cups of coffee, and his head was fuzzy, like he couldn't quite get his mind's antenna aligned right to get his thoughts to come in clear.

Stress, he thought once more. *Stress and...*

The pills. He hated how much he was beginning to suspect the medication was what he really needed. He shouldn't have chosen such a hectic time in their life to try and stop taking them. It was the wrong time to experiment and think he knew better than Dr. Pillsman.

I've got to be better, Declan thought. *For them.*

At the thought of Norah and Knox, Declan walked out into the yard a ways and pulled his cell phone from his pocket. Called Norah, and was disappointed to once again get her voice mail without a single ring.

Phone's still off. They're still on the plane.

Declan tried to remember if their flight plan had included a change of plane somewhere, and how long the layover would be. He figured it probably did, because direct flights were usually more expensive, but at the same time, they might have splurged to cut down on any hassle for Norah since she was traveling with Knox. But that fuzzy static in his mind continued to obscure the details he needed.

He sighed and shoved his phone back into his pocket. Cursed himself for not just hiring a moving company and traveling with his wife and son.

Be in the moment, he told himself. *From today on, you'll be the best father and husband in the world.*

"And there's not a fucking thing you can do about the past except learn from it."

Dr. Pillsman had said this to him on more than one occasion, though she hadn't spruced it up with such colorful language.

Declan's phone chirped in his hand, a single beep indicating a new voice mail. His heart surged with happiness and relief, thinking Norah had managed to call and he'd simply missed it, maybe because of iffy cell signal out here in the country. But when he looked at his screen he saw the message was actually from his next-door neighbor at their old house, Gary Atwood. Gary and Declan had grown to be good friends over the four years since Declan and Norah had moved into the house next to the man. Gary had a penchant for reading, so Declan and he would often share a beer or three on the back porch and discuss books, authors, and occasionally films. Over the last year or so, when things had gotten tough for Declan, he found that Gary Atwood was one of the only people on earth he felt he could trust other than Norah.

Declan tapped the screen to play the message.

Deck, it's Gary. Listen, if you—

A loud screeching sound screamed from the speaker and the voice mail was cut off. Declan winced at the noise and pulled the phone from his ear, looked at the screen and saw that the voice mail had vanished from the list. He shook his head. *Might have to switch phone service out here. One more thing for the list.* He made a mental note to make sure to call Gary as soon as they were settled in to let him know he was always welcome to come visit. Declan would snap a picture of the pond and the dock and let Gary know that the view and the beers would be waiting.

The sun had pushed higher into the sky and the air was growing warmer, the winter chill that had lingered earlier this morning having been forced back into the trees to lick its wounds. The sunlight and clear sky gave the pond a metallic blue tint that seemed to beckon swimmers, and though Declan was having a hard time shaking away the cobwebs in his mind, he was not so far gone to think the weather was suitable for skinny-dipping or any other type of aquatic activity.

However, with the warm sun on his back and the air crisp and clean, he decided that some natural Vitamin D and some good ole-fashioned fresh air might be exactly what he needed to decompress. Those things and some more of that amazing coffee.

Yes, that sounded like just what the doctor ordered.

The U-Haul could wait. Self-care was important, right?

There was no sense in overexerting himself today if it would only lead to him being less effective tomorrow or the day after. Work smarter, not harder, right? Maybe when Norah and Knox landed and she called him, he would tell her to stop at a hotel for the night and then come to the house tomorrow and they could both start the day fresh. He'd tell her to stay someplace nice, not to think twice about the cost.

Declan turned and walked to the back door, stopped when he saw what was imprinted into the flaking paint.

Gray and faded, mostly washed away by countless rainstorms, the boot print looked to be a men's size, maybe ten or eleven, and was placed squarely below the doorknob, exactly where Declan would have tried to strike if he'd been attempting to kick the door open.

Declan stared at the boot print for a full minute, waiting to see if his head would eventually clear and the markings would disappear the same way the Charger had vanished once he'd opened the back door. When the print remained visible, Declan smiled, thinking again of the unknown author of the black book, and the deep inspiration the writer had drawn from this place.

He went inside to make more coffee.

3

Declan filled the kettle and set it to boil on the stove, discarding another used matchstick into the sink basin. The previous cups of coffee he'd consumed were ready to take their exit, so while the water heated he returned to the little bathroom under the stairs and relieved himself. As he did, spreading his legs to slouch down and keep his head from hitting the slanted ceiling, the hair on the back of his neck began to prickle and another chill caused him to shudder, a few droplets of piss splashing over the bowl and onto the floor.

Declan felt like he was being watched. One of those instinctual senses that hit hard and fast, a biological alarm triggered. With this encroaching feeling, Declan's mind went back to Ivan's story, to the vision the doomed man had experienced in the mirror of the bathroom the author had clearly created based on the very one Declan stood in now.

Declan didn't want to turn around. Didn't want to see what might be looking back at him from the cracked glass. Feeling ashamed, like a child who'd watched a scary movie and had to call for their parents in the middle of the night, Declan zipped his pants, flushed the toilet, and sidestepped out of the bathroom without turning around.

As soon as he crossed the threshold and was back in the daylight falling through the house's front windows, the chill of dread that had crept up his spine in the bathroom was erased, like a fever had suddenly broken. The teakettle whistled from the kitchen, and the sound was Pavlovian, making Declan's mouth water for more coffee. He hurried down the hallway and into the kitchen, glancing once to the black book, which still lay open and facedown on the table where he'd dropped it. "Well done," he said to the book. "You've officially managed to creep me out." But he said the words with admiration, an appreciation of the author's craft.

Declan removed the kettle from the stove and made another cup of coffee. He wouldn't swear to it, because when he'd made the first two cups it had been early and he'd still been groggy, but as he put four scoops of instant coffee into the mug, his brain seemed to be trying to tell him something, that something wasn't computing properly. Declan stared into the open coffee can, and he realized what it was. By his calculation, he'd now scooped something like ten or eleven spoonfuls of coffee out of the can, but the level of coffee inside the can didn't seem to be any lower than it had been when Declan had first opened it.

He didn't have long to ponder what he figured was only an optical illusion, because from behind him came a soft rustling noise. Declan spun around with the coffee scoop held out in front of him like a sword, but he saw nothing else in the kitchen. He scanned the room, held his breath and listened. Nothing moved. Nothing made a sound. He sighed, laughed at how pathetic he looked waving the coffee scoop around, and took the first sip of his fresh cup of coffee.

That was when he saw the book had changed.

4

Like with the Charger, again there was no fear. At least not at first. At first, there was only more curiosity. Declan took another small sip of his coffee and stared at the black book on the breakfast table, which was now closed and with its front cover facing up toward the ceiling.

How? Declan wondered. *How did that happen?*

The answer, of course, was that it hadn't—books don't move on their own. But this was now the second time in only an hour or two that Declan had found the book in either a different position or a different location entirely from what he'd remembered last.

And that was when the fear came, not fear of the book, or of the house, or of any silly things going bump in the night or some masked man with a knife hiding in a closet, but fear that he might actually be losing his mind. He'd felt off from the moment he'd awakened in the bedroom upstairs, his memory fuzzy, unable to shake an underlying confusion to all his thoughts and actions. But Declan knew he had sat at that breakfast table and read the story about Ivan. He knew that he'd dropped the book on the table when he'd caught sight of the Dodge Charger outside the back door's window, and it had landed facedown and open.

But you didn't really see the Charger, did you, Deck? his voice of reason asked.

"No," Declan said into his coffee mug. "I didn't."

So maybe you never dropped the book the way you remember. Maybe it was all a—

"A dream?" Declan asked. He rubbed his eyes and patted himself a couple times on the cheek, hard enough to bring some color to it. "Jesus, I'm completely spent."

That was it. That settled it once and for all. No unloading of the truck today. Today was going to be a day to relax and recover and enjoy as much of their new home as he could. He was going to stick to his newly formed plan of enjoying his coffee outside, and he was going to take the black book out with him and read the Ivan story again, try and see what exactly it was about the author's words that had resonated so deeply with him.

Declan plucked the book from the breakfast table and

tucked it under his arm, then walked out the back door and across the yard and made his way to the end of the old dock, any fear from the horrific vision he'd had out there earlier all but forgotten. He sat on the edge with his legs hanging over, the soles of his shoes nearly grazing the water's surface. He took another sip of coffee and then set the mug down beside him.

When he picked up the black book to open it, he saw that the gold letters had somehow reappeared on the front cover.

And they did not say IVAN.

Instead, they offered a new name.

WILLOW

Instead of confusion, instead of fear, this time all Declan felt was the excitement that came along with getting to read a new story. He ran his fingers over the gold letters, and he could feel the charge in them, an energy begging to be released.

He opened the book to the first page and started to read.

Willow was in love, and she thought she might kill for it...

WILLOW

1

Willow was in love, and she thought she might kill for it.

She sat in the Toyota Previa's rear left seat, the old van's air conditioner on full blast, and she glared at Eva's long, tan legs stretching from the front passenger seat. The girl's bare feet were on the dash, toenails painted pink, and Willow squinted hard and concentrated on trying to shoot lasers from her eyes that would slice through Eva's skin and bone and muscle and chop the legs off at the knee. There'd be no blood, because the laser's heat would instantly cauterize the wound. The lower halves of Eva's perfect legs would simply pop off and fall to the floorboard like they'd been plucked from a Mr. Potato Head doll, a department store mannequin disassembled. Willow imagined the scream that would come next. First, Eva's entire body would jolt with the lightning bolt of pain, and for a moment she would make no noise at all because the confusion of what had just happened would render her catatonic while her brain processed images and tried to catch up, but then the sight of her leg pieces crisscrossed on the floorboard where they'd tumbled, the realization that she was looking down at the bottoms of her own bare feet sticking up at her like grotesque weeds growing through cracked asphalt, would reignite her senses and the pain would hit again, brilliant and all-encompassing this time, and the noise she would make then would be a noise that Eva would have previously thought herself incapable of producing. It would deafen them all, threaten to shatter the van's windows.

Willow would smile. Because Eva's scream would be the sound of somebody realizing their perfect life had been snatched away from them in the blink of an eye.

"Dude, you've got that look on your face again." Cesca's voice pulled Willow from her fantasy.

"What look?" Willow asked, turning to look at her best friend seated beside her in the other rear captain's chair.

"You know what look. The one that girl from *Stranger Things* makes right before she makes someone's brain explode. I swear to God, if your nose starts bleeding, I'm going to pass out. You know I hate blood."

Willow rolled her eyes. "I know. I'm amazed you haven't fainted and concussed yourself on a toilet bowl while you change your tampon."

The two girls laughed together, one of a million laughs they'd shared since becoming friends in grade school. Laughter that had grown with them, matured with them from those days in Windy Ridge Elementary's hallways until now, second semester of their freshman year of college.

When the laughter finally faded, Willow noticed Eva turned in her seat, looking back at her and smiling. "What's so funny?"

"Just some TikTok of a guy dancing while his dog looks at him like he's embarrassed," Cesca said, always quick on her feet.

Eva laughed. "Oh, I love those! Dogs' faces are so expressive, right?"

Willow and Cesca muttered in agreement and then Eva asked, "You have enough service to watch TikToks out here?" She pulled her cell phone from the cupholder and checked the screen. "I've had barely a single bar since we got into the trees."

"Uh ... yes. I mean, no. It's been spotty. Guess I had just enough at the time."

Eva nodded and put her phone back in the cupholder.

Willow was checking her own phone screen and seeing that, indeed, she had no service when Vaughn spoke from the driver's seat. "Yeah, that's not too surprising. Way out here in the mountains, hell, folks probably don't even know we've landed on the moon. Probably think cell phones are alien technology."

Eva laughed loud and hard and slapped Vaughn on the knee.

Willow rolled her eyes. Vaughn's joke wasn't that funny. But Vaughn *was* funny. His sense of humor was one of the many things Willow loved about him. The crack about the moon landing wasn't even in his top thousand greatest hits.

Yet Eva had laughed like it was maybe the first joke she'd ever heard. She looked over at her boyfriend and her eyes were alight with...

Love, Willow thought. *She actually fucking loves him. Or at least thinks she does. But how could she? She's only known him, what ... a few months. I've known him since—*

Cesca punched Willow in the shoulder. Mouthed to her, *Be nice.*

Willow sighed and laid her head against the window, watched the trees pass and the sun burst through the gaps in the branches like...

Lasers.

"Vaughn, since I'm teetering on the edge of carsickness back here, before I puke all over the back of Willow's and Cesca's heads can you please tell me where exactly we're going? I don't want to die before the surprise." In the Previa's third row, Cory slid himself into the middle seat and waited for Vaughn to answer. He'd been lying down for the last twenty minutes or so with his headphones on and his eyes closed, and when Willow turned around to look at their friend now, she saw that his face was pale and he had a fine sheen of sweat on his brow and upper lip.

"Vaughn," she said, "I think he really is sick."

Cory tried to smile at her, but it looked pained, and he slumped back into the seat and closed his eyes.

"Not too much longer now, Cor. I promise."

Willow kicked the back of the driver's seat.

"Uh," Vaughn said, glancing up and meeting Willow's eyes in the rearview. "But, hey, do you need me to stop for a few? Pull over so you can get some air?"

Eva turned around and looked back through the middle of the van, saw Cory sprawled out in the back and said, "He really doesn't look good, Vaughn. Pull over."

Willow hated that Eva was also being compassionate toward Cory. Cory was *their* friend, not hers. *They* would look out for him. Didn't need her help.

From the third row, Cory asked, "How much further, Vaughn? Seriously."

Willow watched as Vaughn looked down not at his cell phone in the cupholder next to Eva's, where the GPS showed their location in an ocean of green, slowly following the snakelike line of the road, but to the van's odometer. "For real, like maybe another mile or two."

Cory raised a hand up with his palm out, as if praising some deity, and said, "Continue on, good sir. If I should perish before we arrive, I want you all to know it has been my life's greatest pleasure to—"

"Shut up, nerd," Cesca said. "You've looked worse from a hangover. Plus, as slow as Vaughn's driving, we'd be better off walking."

"Yeah, in this heat?" Vaughn said. "Good luck. And I'm going slow because I don't want to miss the turn. It's not marked. I don't want to—"

Vaughn jumped on the brakes and the van's tires yipped and Willow's seat belt locked and bit painfully into her collarbone, the nylon burning the skin exposed in the cutout of her tank top. Cory fell forward, caught himself on the back of Willow's and Cesca's seats with a gasp and a grunt.

"Sorry!" Vaughn said, swiveling in his seat, a curl of his

sandy-blond hair falling into his eyes. He pushed it away and glanced at each of them, taking inventory. "All good?"

The three of them in the back nodded and said they were fine.

Vaughn turned to Eva and put a hand on her knee. With a softened voice he asked, "You okay, babe?"

Willow thought she'd beat Cory to the punch and blow chunks all over the back of the van.

Eva smiled and nodded. "I'm fine," she said, waving a hand dismissively, as if even she was a bit put off by Vaughn's syrupy concern. She pulled her feet from the dash and sat up straight, looking out the windshield. "What happened?"

Vaughn cleared his throat and then turned and looked ahead. He pointed to the left, to a small gap in the trees that looked like the start of what might have once been a service road but had been long since decommissioned. "I think that's our turn."

The five of them stared at the would-be road for ten seconds of wary silence. Finally, Cory called from the back row, "Did we run out of gas?"

"What?" Vaughn said. "No, of course not."

It was Eva who laughed, and Vaughn shot her a look.

"He's telling you to drive," Eva said.

"Oh," Vaughn said. "Right. Sorry."

He drove the van forward and slowly made the turn, and Willow felt like she was the only one who realized that in those few seconds of silence and stillness before Cory had spoken, it seemed Vaughn was suddenly wondering if he'd made the wrong call, and they all should have gone to the beach instead.

2

Willow and Cesca met in the third grade, and Vaughn moved in down the block from Willow four years later, right as the all-important transition from elementary to middle school was taking place. The first day Willow saw him standing on the corner of the sidewalk, waiting for the bus with the rest of the kids, she felt the instant slap of infatuation across her face.

Vaughn was tall for his age, standing a full head over the rest of the boys headed off to the first day of middle school, and the way he leaned against the light pole with his hands in his pockets and his blue Jansport slung over one shoulder, his eyes bright and alert, a permanent smirk on his lips as he watched and listened to everyone around him, made it seem like he was already the king of the seventh grade.

When the bus arrived, Vaughn let all the other kids pile on first before he pushed himself off the light pole and made his languid strides up the steps. Willow's heart raced in her chest when she realized that she had no one sitting next to her, and there was a chance Vaughn would choose her bench as his seat.

He did, and Willow quickly turned and looked out the window, afraid that if she looked into Vaughn's eyes she might combust.

"Hi," Vaughn said. "I'm Vaughn. I'm the new guy everybody's been staring at."

Willow, realizing she was going to have to speak or pretend to be deaf and mute, managed to squeak out, "I'm Willow. Nice to meet you," the formal and practiced way she'd been taught to greet friends of her parents when they had company over.

Still looking out the bus window, Willow could practically feel the smirk on Vaughn's face grow bigger, and she wished she *could* combust, so she wouldn't have to suffocate in her own embarrassment.

"Pleasure is all mine, Willow. Any tips for a guy's first day at a new school?"

At twelve years old, Willow had no great insight into the world, and was in fact dealing with her own anxiety at attending a new school. Sixth graders were on top of the world in elementary school—the *big* kids—but seventh graders were right back down at the bottom of the ladder. Willow decided to be honest. "It's my first day of middle school, too," she said.

"Ah." Vaughn nodded his head. And then he said the thing that made Willow's heart soar. "Well, I guess we'll just have to figure it all out together."

And to Willow's great surprise, they did. She and Cesca, having not had a single class together before lunch, were seated at a round table in the corner of the loud cafeteria with their heads together while Willow was gushing about her encounter with the new boy, Vaughn, when he actually showed up right in front of them. He was holding his lunch tray in one hand—it was chicken patties for lunch that day, Willow would never forget—and smiling at them when they finally pulled their heads apart and realized he was there.

"Can I sit with you all?" he asked.

Willow and Cesca froze, silently staring. Willow's mind raced with what possible sequence of events could have led Vaughn to be forced to sit with *them* at lunch. They weren't social outcasts by any means, but they certainly didn't consider themselves to be in the *popular* group of girls—though with the great social reset of switching from elementary to middle school, Willow supposed the pieces simply hadn't all fallen where they would lie yet—and when she let her eyes look past Vaughn, she saw three other tables mostly full of boys all staring at them, probably wondering just what in the hell the tall new guy was up to.

"Of course," Cesca finally said, elbowing Willow back to the moment. "Willow was just telling me about you."

Willow's face was engulfed in flames. Hot embarrassment threatening to burn down the entire cafeteria.

Cesca snickered, and Willow shot her a death stare.

Vaughn set his tray down and then sat. "Yeah, she saved me a seat on the bus this morning and we have agreed to decipher the meaning of middle school existence together."

Vaughn smiled, Cesca laughed, Willow grinned, feeling the heat begin to drain from her face, and that was the first time the three of them were all together.

Cory was the late addition to the group, moving to Windy Ridge during their sophomore year of high school when his dad had been transferred for work. Cesca was actually the one to bond with Cory first, the two of them getting assigned as lab partners in Mr. Eckes's biology class, and when she brought him over to meet them at Vaughn's house after school that afternoon, it was a done deal. Cory quickly became one of them.

Willow was still the shy one, the one who wore Converse sneakers and horror movie and band t-shirts and applied the minimum amount of makeup. Cesca was more into the girly stuff, always shopping for new outfits, loved reality television shows full of hot, shirtless guys. Cory was thin and lanky, a few inches shorter than Vaughn, and had brown hair that he always let get too long before getting it trimmed. His fashion choices were more aligned with Willow—t-shirts and hoodies and cargo shorts with a battered pair of Vans he would wear until the soles wore out. He liked music and video games and indie films. Vaughn had grown bigger and broader, standing right at six foot three and with shoulders that made him a prime target of the high school football coach's recruiting efforts. But Vaughn didn't play sports in school. He liked exercising and he enjoyed playing just about anything that involved a ball for fun, but he never joined a school team, saying he'd rather have his time to himself and didn't want the pressure of success.

God, how Willow loved him for that.

How she loved everything about him.

The four of them were very different in a lot of ways, and Willow knew that they all loved each other to a certain degree. Knew that they all understood that what the four of them shared was something special, something not every person in life gets to experience. But despite all the years that had passed them by, despite all the changes that had come along with growing from children to teenagers to legal adults together, every time Willow looked at Vaughn and caught that smirk on his face, she was still that twelve-year-old girl on the sidewalk, and he was still the same boy who'd leaned against the light pole and watched the rest of them like the whole world amused him. The boy who'd sat next to her on the bus and told her they'd figure it all out together.

She'd always loved him, and she'd never done a single thing about it. In fact, in a pure triumph over the odds, none of the four of them had ever dated or so much as shared a single kiss with each other. They'd all had boyfriends and girlfriends off and on through high school, but nothing had ever lasted more than a few months. In the end, they all seemed to just prefer hanging out with each other.

When they all ended up going to the little state college two hours from their hometown, something inside Willow told her that the time was coming, that soon she and Vaughn would realize the feelings between them. But first semester had been tough for all of them, learning their new routines and responsibilities and juggling course loads that made their high school days feel like preschool. When they'd all been home for Christmas break and had started discussing their Spring Break plans, Willow thought the trip would be the perfect time for things between her and Vaughn to go to the next level.

But then Eva had walked into Vaughn's Intro to Economics class and everything had gone to shit.

3

"I thought you said it was only another mile or two," Cory said from the third row. He was sitting up straighter now, the toes of his Vans popping into the peripheral of Willow's vision. She glanced back at him and saw that his face had more color to it than it had back on the main road, and his eyes didn't look as glazed over. His carsickness must have passed.

Which Willow guessed made sense, because ever since Vaughn had turned off that curving road and squeezed the van into the tree-encroached path—because as tight and narrow as it was, Willow didn't think it deserved any more of a designation than *path*—the sun had been mostly blotted out by the overhanging branches of the tall trees, helping to cool the temperature, and the road had seemed to be as straight as an arrow for what had felt like miles. Speaking of which...

"That's what I thought we had left until the turn-off," Vaughn said from the front. He had both hands on the wheel, and Willow had been watching him in the rearview mirror for the last several minutes, noted the way his eyes kept flicking up to it, as if checking to see if somebody was following them. There was an uneasy look in those eyes—Willow had known him long enough to recognize it—and it further reinforced what Willow had thought back before they'd made the turn ... that Vaughn thought coming here might have been the wrong idea. "I'm ... I'm not sure how long we follow this road," he added. And maybe he recognized his own apprehension in his voice and didn't like the sound of it, didn't want the others to notice he was second-guessing himself, because he perked up a little then and said, "But I assure you our private oasis will be waiting for us very soon."

Cesca looked over to Willow and they shared a look—Cesca having known Vaughn long enough too, understanding that their friend didn't sound like this very often. Willow shrugged and decided to help pick up the vibe inside the van by gently ribbing Vaughn a little. "This place better be fucking paradise, Vaughn. Cesca and I could be poolside right now at the beach, sipping virgin daiquiris and flirting with cabana boys."

Willow saw Vaughn grin in the rearview—that smirk that she loved—and from behind her Cory said, "The place we were going to stay had, like, one and a half stars and looked like a giant cinder block. I assure you the nightly rate did not include poolside cabanas, nor cabana boys. I'm not even sure it included towels and pillows."

Cesca laughed, Willow joined in, and from the front seat Eva added, "Gotta love being a broke college student."

"True dat," Cesca said, still smiling.

"Amen," Cory said.

Willow said nothing, rolling her eyes. She knew Eva was only playing along. The girl was a lot of things, but broke wasn't one of them.

"See," Vaughn said, "you all should be thanking me for saving us some money and not tossing it away to spend a week in some shithole that's price-gauging college kids who just want to come have some fun for a few days."

Which was sort of true. Despite Cesca's quips and jokes, they had collectively eventually decided that a week spent at an overcrowded beach town, surrounded by a million other college students, wasn't exactly the relaxing retreat they were looking for. They'd opted for this weekend trip instead, before heading home to see their family the rest of the week. But Willow knew the truth of the matter. If not for her...

"Fair enough," Cesca said. "Thanks, Vaughn. Thanks for locking us all in your van and driving for hours without telling us where the hell we're going. I mean, come to think of it, this is essentially kidnapping."

"I'd call the cops," Cory said, "but still no service."

Vaughn shot them the finger. "Who do I call about carrying a load of whiny bitches?"

The three of them in the back laughed some more, but Eva slapped Vaughn's shoulder. "*Vaughn.*"

Vaughn smiled at her, a full-on display of teeth. "*What?*" he asked, playfully rubbing his arm.

"I can assure you he has called us much worse," Cory said.

Vaughn laughed and nodded. "And you deserved it each and every time."

"*Well...,*" Cesca started.

"That's debatable," Cory added.

"Oh," Vaughn said, "like you all haven't had some choice words for—*hey, look!*"

He stepped on the brakes again, and once more the tires locked up and this time Cory didn't quite manage to catch himself on the back of Willow and Cesca's seats, and he tumbled into the gap between their chairs, falling to his knees.

The van was silent again for half a second, each of them doing a quick inventory of themselves, and then Cory said, "That's it, I'm walking the rest of the way. Vaughn is clearly having some sort of stroke up there. I'd rather take my chance as a hitchhiker at this point."

Eva snorted a laugh, and this time Willow couldn't help but join in. Cesca reached out a hand and helped Cory get up and back into his seat.

"Very funny, asshole," Vaughn said. "But you're too late. We're already there."

Vaughn pointed straight ahead through the windshield, and Willow and Cesca tilted their heads toward each other to see out. Willow could feel Cory's breath hot on the back of her neck as he leaned forward to get a look, and it made her shiver. About twenty yards ahead, the tree line did not widen, but simply ended, as if a great scythe had swept across the land and made a clean slice through the forest. Beyond the opening, the air shimmered with the heat of the afternoon sun in the cloudless sky, making the old two-story farmhouse that sat at the end of the gravel road look like a mirage that might not hold out long enough for them to finish the drive. The grass was mostly dead and burnt, but the trees all around them and mountains in the far-off distance popped with vibrant and deep shades of green.

It was Eva who broke the silence. "Vaughn ... this is ... weird."

Cory leaned in closer still, and Willow could smell his deodorant. "Hey, Vaughn, is that the house that fell on the Wicked Witch of the West?"

"East," Willow said. "The house fell on the Wicked Witch of the East."

"Oh, shit. Yeah, you're right. Does that make us tied again?"

Willow nodded. "Yep. You just gave away your lead."

The two film buffs of the group, Willow and Cory had been playing an unofficial movie trivia game between them for years.

Vaughn was driving again now, the Previa popping out of the tree line like somebody had spat out a kidney bean. The sun blasted back through the windshield again and the air conditioner whined in protest.

Willow looked over to Cesca and saw that now she was the one who looked uneasy. "Seriously, Vaughn, what is this place?" Cesca asked.

Willow caught another of Vaughn's smirks in the rearview, and it seemed as though now that they'd actually found the place, any apprehension he'd been feeling before had left his mind. "Just wait until you see what's around back," Vaughn said.

Eva glanced from Vaughn, out the windshield to the house, and then back to her boyfriend. "Care to give us a hint?"

Willow thought the girl sounded a bit afraid, as if Eva was letting the reality of the situation sink in fully. That she'd climbed into a van full of people she hardly knew at all—Vaughn included—and now they were driving up to some dilapidated old house in the middle of nowhere.

We're a satanic cult, for all you know, Willow thought. *And you'll make a lovely sacrifice.*

"Like I said," Vaughn said, patting Eva's knee, "our own private oasis."

He drove the van right up to the home's front porch and

parked, killing the engine, the air conditioner quieting down to nothing with a sad sigh of relief.

4

After being shut off, the Previa's engine ticked like a bomb was about to go off under the van's hood. With no air conditioner providing even the tiniest relief from the scorching sun, the inside of the van quickly began to feel like a sauna, a thick, heavy heat filling the space like a poisonous gas. But for another thirty seconds or so after Vaughn had parked the van, all five of them stared out the windshield at the old house, nobody speaking. Willow figured the rest of them were probably wondering if Vaughn was trying to play some sort of half-assed joke, but she knew he wasn't. This was the place. Exactly where they were supposed to be.

This was the place she'd tell Vaughn she loved him, and she hoped—no, she *knew*, she could *feel* it—that he'd tell her the same.

"I'm not entirely sure what the symptoms of heatstroke are," Cory said, passing between Willow and Cesca's seats and reaching for the sliding door's handle, "but if I don't get out of this van, I'm sure I'll get to have a firsthand experience." He pulled the door open and even though it was at least eighty-five degrees outside, the air that rushed into the van might as well have been ice water for the comfort it brought. A breeze came in and examined them all and its sudden presence prickled Willow's arms with goose bumps, making her shiver.

Vaughn popped open the driver's door and called to

Cory, "Carsick, heatstroke, damn, Cor, pick an ailment and stick with it."

Willow and Cesca grinned at each other and then filed out of the back of the van, just as Eva stepped out of the front passenger seat. The three girls formed a line alongside Cory, who was standing back from the van so he could look up at the front of the house. He was shielding his eyes against the sun's glare, and Willow caught the little smile twitch across his face.

"I know what you're thinking," she said, bumping his shoulder. "*Cabin in the Woods*?"

Cory shook his head. "Good one, but no. I was thinking older." He chinned toward the house. "It's got more of a *Texas Chain Saw* vibe to it."

"Either way, you're fucked," Willow said and bumped his shoulder again.

"You're right. Vaughn and I are goners. There's never the Final Guy, always a girl. We don't stand a chance. So ... good luck to you."

"Luck? Have you seen these two wimps?" Willow said, pointing to Eva and Cesca. "My fate is sealed. I'll be the one back at some run-down police station in town explaining all your gruesome deaths, no doubt at all."

"I admire your confidence."

"I've had a lifetime of preparation for this moment. Time to put all I've learned to use."

Cory shrugged. "I've had the same training, but I was cursed with a penis."

Willow laughed. "A guy's dick will always be his downfall."

Cesca, who'd apparently been letting Willow and Cory have their secret little horror nerd moment, chimed in: "Maybe, but it *does* have at least one use I find enjoyable."

Eva, who'd been standing a few feet away from them all, watching Vaughn walk around the back of the Previa and pop the back hatch, smiled and said, "Now *that* we can agree on." She gave Cesca a high five, and to Willow's dismay, Cesca laughed too and actually high-fived the girl back. When Cesca saw the look Willow was giving her, all she did was shrug and shake her head.

"Not exactly what I imagined," Cory said. "But you got to admit..." He turned and grinned at Willow. "It's very creepy, and very fucking cool." He moved around her, walking over to help Vaughn with their luggage and supplies.

Willow called after him, "Just remember, it's all fun and games until you hear the chainsaw."

There was a big Yeti cooler in the back of the van, and Cory lifted the lid and pulled a can of beer from the ice—the beer and other alcohol were courtesy of upperclassmen who would gladly supply needy underage students with whatever their thirsty little hearts desired ... for a hefty markup, of course. Cory popped the tab, took a sip, sighed in satisfaction, and said, "If these are my last moments before getting ripped to shreds, you better believe I'm going to enjoy them."

Vaughn grabbed a beer for himself, popped it open, and clinked his can against Cory's. "That's a weird cheers, but yeah ... here's to enjoying ourselves."

Willow and Cesca walked over to the back of the van, and Cory handed them each a White Claw from the cooler, the cans flecked with frost and chips of ice. Cesca pressed the can to her forehead, and Willow rested hers against the back of her neck. Cold dripped down the back of her tank top, slicing down her spine, and she shivered in pleasure and looked up to meet Vaughn's eyes, wanted to fall into them, wanted him to catch her.

But Vaughn wasn't looking at her. Was instead looking past her, past all of them, back to where Eva was still standing, several feet back from the van, the girl's hand up above her eyes, shielding them from the sun as she stared at one of the old house's upper windows. She looked frozen, her body rigid and her lips open and rounded like she was trying to whistle. Then, just as a breeze skirted over the treetops and blessed them with its coolness, Eva jumped back, her body alive again, as if jolted awake from a nightmare.

"Eva?" Vaughn said, already moving toward his girlfriend, pushing past Willow as though she wasn't even there.

The three of them still standing by the van's opened back hatch all turned in unison and watched as Vaughn reached Eva and put a hand on her shoulder.

"Hey, are you okay?"

Eva's eyes flitted up to that second-story window again, then glanced once to the three of them standing by the van, and then her eyes finally settled on Vaughn. "Where did you say you found this place?" she asked.

"Uhh ... online," Vaughn stammered.

Eva nodded. "And there's not supposed to be anybody else here, right?"

5

"I'm telling you, Vaughn, I saw people inside. I mean ... sort of." Eva had joined them all at the back of the van now, and Cory had held out a can of beer and a White Claw to her. She'd taken the beer from him but she'd yet to open it.

Vaughn was nodding, and Willow found she loved the smirk on his face, because it looked like he was doing nothing but placating Eva by pretending to take her concern seriously. "Okay, okay," Vaughn said. "But what do you mean by 'sort of'? I mean, somebody is either there or they aren't, right?"

All heads swiveled toward Eva, curious.

Eva sighed and looked up into the bright, clear sky, closed her eyes and took a deep breath. Willow couldn't tell if the girl was realizing and coming to terms with how silly she sounded or if she was trying to calm herself down because she was frustrated that the people she was traveling with were too stupid to understand what she meant. Willow didn't really care which of those two options was the truth, but she did hate the fact that they'd only been at the house for a few minutes and already Eva was stealing all the attention for herself.

It was Cory who finally reached out and touched Eva's wrist, causing the girl's eyes to open slowly and then look down and meet his. "Just tell us," Cory said, his voice calm and sympathetic. "We won't think you're crazy or anything, I promise. Willow and I have already discussed how this house is clearly a horror movie relic, right, Willow?"

Willow felt a quick flash of anger that Cory would invite

Eva into their private world, but she forced on a smile and nodded, making herself take one for the team—for *Vaughn*, really—and said, "Totally."

It was Willow's words that finally seemed to bring Eva's mind back to the group, as if having another female on her side was worth more than all the guys.

If you only knew how much I wish Leatherface would come for you first, Willow thought, imagining Eva's guts getting tangled in the chainsaw blade, but she kept that stupid smile on her face so long her face started to hurt. She could feel the sweat trickling down her lower back and into her shorts, and while Eva started to talk, Willow found herself focusing not so much on the girl's words as on the way her long legs seemed to stretch forever, bronzed and elegant, the way Eva's tank top seemed to crave hugging her in all the right places while her blond hair danced in the breeze, a mesmerizing routine meant to cause sailors to crash their ships upon the rocky shore.

Sorry, Barbie, Willow thought. *Only one of us is leaving here with him, and you're going to need a lot more than your tits and ass to win this war.*

But when Willow looked over to Vaughn and saw that he was now leaning against the back of the van with his arms crossed, nodding along as Eva explained, the placating smirk gone from his face and replaced with what looked like genuine concern, she felt the first inklings of doubt begin to creep back into her psyche. Doubts that had kept her from telling Vaughn how she really felt for so long that she had finally worked up the strength and confidence to squelch down and bury away and hide from herself. The feeling startled her, shook her, and she looked to Cesca and Cory for some reassurance. She got none, because a quick look around the group and Willow saw that *all* of her friends were fully committed to Eva's story. Willow rolled her eyes and joined them in paying attention, but not before taking a long swig from her drink, hoping a little buzz would dull her irritation ... or maybe help her embrace it.

"And at first I thought it was just one of your guys' reflections, right?" Eva said, nodding to Vaughn and Cory. "It had to be."

"In the bottom window?" Cesca asked.

Eva nodded, and her big blue eyes seemed to have grown even larger and more piercing. "Yes. Right there." She pointed past the van to a window a few yards to the left of the front door. "I thought it was just a weird trick of the sun, like, the glare or something. But then I noticed that you three were *right next* to me, and Vaughn was already behind the van, opening the back, completely out of view from that window. So, no way it was him. Plus ... Vaughn was moving —you know, opening the back, shuffling things around, pulling the cooler forward. But the guy in the window ... he was just ... *staring*. Just watching."

"Watching what?" Cesca asked.

Eva shrugged. "Us?"

Nobody said anything, and Willow figured they were all imagining some creeper spying on them from inside the old house, a homeless guy, perhaps, a squatter, or ... *Or some guy in a big rain slicker who likes to hang people from meat hooks in the basement.*

"It freaked me out, because for a second it ... it's like the whole world flashed dark."

Oh God, she's really laying it on thick now, Willow thought.

"Dark?" Cesca asked. "Like you couldn't see? Like you were about to pass out? That might be the heat. We should get you out of the sun."

Eva shook her head. "No, not like that. It was ... I swear, guys, I know how this sounds, but it was like all of a sudden I was standing out here but it was nighttime. The moon was in the sky and the guy was still right there in the window, just staring. He looked ... he looked scared."

"You could tell that from all the way over there?" Willow chimed in, pointing back to where Eva had been standing.

Eva nodded. "Yeah, but..." She trailed off, looked at Willow like she was trying to decide if she really wanted to say what was on her mind. In the end, she looked around the rest of the group and just said, "Yeah. I could tell."

Cory cleared his throat, used his thumb to point up over his shoulder. "But you were looking at one of the upstairs windows when you, uh, got startled and Vaughn ran over to you."

Eva still hadn't opened her beer, but now she fiddled with the pull tab, her pink nails plucking it a few times before she pressed the can to her forehead the same way Cesca had done and rubbed it back and forth, leaving behind a windowpane of condensation on her skin. She looked down to the grass, her stare growing vacant as she slipped back into the memory. "Everything changed just as fast as it had before." Without looking up from the ground, she snapped her finger. "Just like that. The sun was back, but it was behind me now, and everything looked more ... gray. Like everything was dead.

"Something moved in the window up there." She still didn't pull her stare from the grass, but she nodded up, ever so slightly toward the house's second story. "So I looked and ... I saw the guy there."

"He was in the upstairs window now?" Cory asked, cocking his head, looking like he was desperately trying to understand.

Eva shook her head. "No. I mean, yes. I mean..." She sighed. "There was a different guy in the upstairs window. He looked a little older than the other guy. He looked tired and ... I jumped because all of a sudden he looked down toward where the van was parked, tilted his whole head down this way, and when I got a better look I..." Eva stopped and laughed, as if finally, after spewing all this craziness to them, she was realizing it was all ridiculous and none of what she was saying could have really happened and that Cesca was probably right and it was just the heat that was messing with her head, making her delirious.

It was Cory again now, the one of them who wasn't quite ready to write her story off. "What?" he asked. "What happened when he looked down?"

Eva took a deep breath and looked up, glanced to the upstairs window, as if checking to make sure nobody was still watching, needing there to be nobody there before she could bring herself to finish. Willow and Cesca's gaze followed Eva's up to the window, and even Vaughn stood from the back of the van and turned to take a peek himself.

But Cory stayed where he was, patient and waiting. Nobody saw anything in the upstairs window, of course.

"I thought I recognized him," Eva said. "I have no idea who he was, but I swear I'd seen him before."

With Eva's story apparently over, the five of them fell into a pocket of silence, the air shimmering with heat all around them, begging for another breeze. Willow waited, knowing she didn't have to be the one to say the whole thing sounded crazy, that Vaughn's girlfriend clearly needed to be on some sort of medication, because surely her friends would be just as in tune.

Her heart dropped when it was Vaughn who finally got things moving again, when he pulled open the cooler and dug through the beer cans and his hand emerged with a bottle of water. He took Eva's unopened beer can from her and placed it back in the cooler, trading her for the water. "Here," he said, unscrewing the top and waiting while she took a long gulp. "Whatever happened, I think we all need to get out of the sun for a few." He pulled her under the shade of the van's opened hatch and then motioned for Cory to follow him. "Come on, Cor, let's go check the place out. Just in case."

As Cory nodded and pushed himself off the van, Willow rolled her eyes and grabbed Cesca's hand, following the boys as they headed for the house. "Some of us aren't damsels in distress," she said, hoping her words struck Eva in the throat. "We're coming too."

As the four of them climbed the warped and sagging porch steps, Willow cursed under her breath when she realized Eva was right behind them, following them into the house.

You won't beat me, she thought. *I promise you that.*

6

Vaughn grabbed the doorknob, a tarnished brass ball that gave a shrill squeak when he turned it, but then stopped before pushing open the door. He looked over his shoulder at the rest of them huddled behind him and said, "Okay, listen … if there really is anybody in here, I think we should—"

"Stay calm and not overreact," Cory said. "Could be a homeless guy, probably more afraid of us than we are of him."

"Or…," Willow said, happy to get to riff off her thoughts from earlier, "it could be an escaped patient from a hush-hush mental hospital hidden back in these woods. You know, the type of place the locals don't like to talk about. And if that's the case, the real question is why was he locked away in the first place? What urges has he been denied all these years? What's he willing to do now that he's free?"

Willow was hoping for Cory to join in on the fun, propose his own slasher theory. Instead, he quickly looked at Eva and said, "She's kidding."

Cesca turned and gave Willow a stern look. Mouthed, *Knock it off.*

In response to this, Willow said in a voice colder than she had meant, "Just open the stupid door, Vaughn."

Vaughn looked at all of them once more, then pushed the door open and stepped inside.

"Hello!" he called out. "Anybody here?"

Cory followed next and said, "Have you, like, *never* seen a horror movie? People who do what you just did usually don't last very long."

Vaughn held up his hands. "I thought you said Willow was kidding about all that."

"Yeah, I mean, she was. But still..." Cory looked at Willow and smiled, gave a little shake of his head, as if saying, *Can you believe this noob?* "Doesn't mean we have to just, you know, ignore *all* the rules of horror films. We don't have to announce our presence to the guy with the big knife, or"—he shrugged—"the demons."

Vaughn groaned. "Christ, now we're talking about demons? Pick a genre, dude."

"There's no demons," Cesca said from beside Willow. "Because if this was Hell or if there was, like, a portal to Hell or something in here, it wouldn't be so damn cool in here. This is ... this is more like Heaven."

Cesca was right, Willow realized, it *was* cool inside the house. Way cooler than it should have been considering the temperature outside and that she very much doubted this home had central A/C. It was stuffy, sure, so much so that if you stuck out your tongue you might be able to lap the air up, but it was definitely cool, at least fifteen degrees cooler than the unseasonably hot spring air they'd just stepped in from.

"Wow, that's wild," Cory said, looking around the space and then up to the ceiling, like he might discover the source of the coolness.

"Place must be insulated like crazy," Vaughn said, adding

his pragmatic wisdom. "Hey, my grandpa always says they don't build things like they used to."

"I wish your shitty van had been built like this house," Cory said. "I lost five pounds of water weight sweating in that back seat."

Vaughn punched Cory in the shoulder, all thoughts of homeless drifters or escaped mental patients apparently forgotten, and Willow and Cesca laughed, giggling in a way that felt much needed to Willow after her longtime friend's repeated defense of Eva.

As the group's laughter faded into the house's walls, Willow cocked her head to the side, catching something in the air, a sort of shift that brought with it a familiar yet somewhat foreign smell. "Hey...," she said, her brain following the trail, trying to land on what it was her nose had picked up. "Do you guys smell that? It smells like ... coffee."

Vaughn and Cory and Cesca all tilted their heads up, sniffing like a pack of hunting dogs. Willow watched as in unison all three of them made a face and shook their heads.

"Nope," Vaughn said. "All I smell is stale air and maybe some mildew."

"Same," Cory said, "And something metallic. Probably rust, or something in the water."

Cesca looked at Willow and shrugged her shoulders. "Sorry. No coffee."

Cory laughed. "There's a plot twist I wouldn't have seen coming. Our would-be slasher greeting us with coffee and pastries before he slices our—"

"Hey! Where's Eva?"

Willow and Cesca were closest to the door, and they turned around and followed the boys' stares around the small foyer and outside onto the porch.

"Eva?" Vaughn called, moving now, pushing between Cesca and Willow to poke his head out the doorway and scan the front yard. Willow couldn't suppress the glee she felt at the fact that when the four of them had fallen into their familiar and comfortable rhythm with each other, they'd *all* —even Vaughn—temporarily forgotten that Eva even existed.

"Over here." Eva's voice was just above a whisper, and they all turned and found her in a room to the left of the foyer, sitting on a faded green couch, looking down at her lap. The entryway to the room was wide and tall, and lined with intricately detailed trim and crown molding along the sides and top. Vaughn and Cory and Cesca walked into the room and stood near Eva, but Willow found her eyes drawn to the design in the trim, stepping closer and running her finger over the carvings. On her closer inspection, the pattern carved into the wood appeared to be a forest of sorts. Lots of trees and leaves and stray branches woven together, forming a continuous, never-ending tapestry of foliage.

But...

Willow leaned closer still, squinted her eyes, ran her index finger over certain areas of the wood again, trying to put tactile truth to what she thought she was seeing.

The carvings outlining the room were not moving, of course not, but it was as if they changed their shapes in Willow's vision depending on the angle she was looking, shifted in her peripheral, falling in and out of focus, playing hide-and-seek with their secrets. Willow was only able to catch fleeting glimpses at a time, darting her eyes left and right as if trying to catch the carvings off guard, surprise them in the act. Finally, she gave up, but what she thought she'd seen in the trim gave the horror nerd in her a tingle of pleasure. Sometimes, those stray branches in the pattern weren't branches at all but long, skinny limbs of some unknown creature, tipped with curved talons. And the big leaves that appeared to be added at random throughout the trees ... they were eyes, wide open and all-seeing.

Watching.

"What's that?" Vaughn's voice pulled Willow away from the pattern, ushered her into the room, which appeared to be the home's living room. It was empty except for a fireplace on the far wall, and the ugly green couch where Eva was seated with everyone else circling her. There was something black in Eva's lap, the object that Vaughn was pointing at and questioning.

Willow joined her friends on the end of the semicircle they formed around Eva, her knees bumping the arm of the couch, dust puffing and then settling to the floor. She looked down and saw a black book in Eva's lap, bound in old leather with red stitching. The cover was blank, and Eva was rubbing her finger across the front the same way Willow had rubbed her finger across the carvings in the wooden trim, searching for something not there.

"Eva?" Vaughn said again, a little more oomph in his voice.

Eva looked up, acted as if she were only seeing them all there for the very first time. Her eyes cleared and she looked down at the book again quickly and then back to them, standing from the couch and holding the book up for them to see. "Just some old book, I guess. Must have been a journal or something that was never used, because the pages are blank. It was sitting just there." She turned and pointed behind her, to the windowsill the couch butted up against. "It was propped up against the glass, like it was ... like it was looking out."

"Maybe your imaginary friend was reading it before we showed up," Willow said and waited for laughter that never came. Received only another round of glances her direction before everyone looked back to Eva.

Cory held out his hand for the book, and Eva gave it to him. Vaughn and Cesca were still watching Eva, but Willow watched as Cory fanned through the book's pages, which were indeed blank as far as Willow could see.

"Maybe it was a kid's," Cory said. "Maybe they wrote in it with invisible ink or something. You remember that stuff? We made it in my science class in, like, I don't know, second or third grade. Thought it was the coolest thing in the world at the time. Like we could send secret messages to all our friends."

"Or," Vaughn said, taking the book from Cory and tossing it onto the couch, another puff of dust, "it's just an old journal that never got used, like Eva said."

Cory shrugged. "Seems awfully worn to have never been used. Looks like somebody's read it a hundred times."

Vaughn shot Cory a look.

"Uh, but, yeah, it's probably just old ... like the rest of this place," Cory said. "Why are we here again?"

Cesca put her hands on her hips. "I'm with Cory. Forget the stupid book, what's the deal, Vaughn?"

Vaughn put his arm around Eva, pulled her close. The girl seemed to melt into him, and the jealousy that flooded Willow was electric. "Okay, okay," Vaughn said, using a hand to rub Eva's upper arm. He was smiling big, like a showman about to perform a trick. "Time for the big reveal. Follow me," he said and broke apart the circle of friends and left the room, reaching the foyer and then glancing to his left down the hallway before turning and heading that direction.

Cesca and Cory followed. Willow stayed behind a moment, giving the black book on the couch cushion a long look that seemed to grow talons of its own. Hooks that sank into the book's blank cover and pulled her toward it, drawing her into its pages.

"Willow?"

Willow jerked her head around, saw Cory waiting in the foyer, motioning for her to join him. She didn't look back to the crown molding as she left the room, but in her head she would swear she could hear the tree limbs rustling as they shape-shifted, those big leaves that were really all-seeing eyes watching her until she turned and disappeared down the hallway.

7

Willow made her way through the kitchen, a shaft of light spilling from the open back door between an old fridge and stove, guiding her way, dust motes parting and spinning lazily away in the sunlight as she disturbed their space.

"Now that's what I'm talking about!" Cesca said as Willow stepped outside, having to raise her hand against the brightness, the heat slapping her across the cheeks.

"Right? I told you it would be worth it," Vaughn said. "Our own private oasis. Would old Vaughn ever let you down?"

"Only when you refer to yourself in the third person," Cory said.

Vaughn ignored him, put his arm around Eva. "What do you think, babe? Perfect, right?"

Vaughn and Eva were standing ahead of the rest of them, Willow having taken her place next to Cesca, who was standing next to Cory a few yards from the house. The backyard sloped slightly downward and eventually led to a great pond, its water a sparkling blue as it reflected the nearly cloudless sky. A small dock and rowboat waited patiently for use, and in the distance more mountains loomed on the horizon, their peaks capping above the tree line that surrounded the entire yard.

Vaughn cocked his head to the side, and Willow saw his smile falter the tiniest bit when Eva didn't immediately answer his question and was instead craning her neck around to look across the yard and take in the sight of the pond with a look somewhere between skepticism and worry.

"Babe?" Vaughn asked again.

There was a flicker of change in Eva's face, and she quickly turned and met Vaughn's stare, her radiant smile popping into place so unexpectedly and practiced it reminded Willow of the way celebrities could always smile on command for selfies with fans or red carpet photo walks.

On and off, like a switch. "It's beautiful," Eva said. "I can't wait to go swimming," she added, giving her words a bit more gusto, which made Willow think the girl was faking her enthusiasm.

I wonder what else she fakes? Willow wondered but then had to quickly push away any images this thought brought to mind.

"Amen to that!" Cesca said. "It's gotta be a hundred degrees out here."

Vaughn turned away from Eva, and Willow watched as he took a deep breath, his strong shoulders rising and falling. He stood there, staring out across the yard and water, silent and unmoving. The three of them—Willow, Cesca, and Cory—all turned and looked at each other, years of friendship stirring the recognition of this moment between them, their thoughts unspoken but perfectly in sync. The realization of what had caused Vaughn to be drawn to this place was now so obvious to those who knew him.

But...

"Vaughn? What's wrong?" It was Eva, stepping closer to Vaughn and reaching up to his cheek with a gentle hand.

Vaughn shook his head and laughed, taking her hand and kissing it—which was *another* image Willow didn't want—and then turned around to face them all, his eyes wet with the prospect of tears. He took another breath and said, "Reminds me of my grandfather's place. How we used to go fishing out on his little boat."

Cory nodded. "Up by Lake Cedar Ridge, right?"

"Where you once reeled in that pair of ladies' underwear and your grandfather told you to give them a whiff and see if they smelled fishy," Cesca tossed on, making them all laugh.

"You went every summer," Willow added, not looking at Vaughn but staring at Eva, letting her know that no matter how close she thought she might be to Vaughn, the rest of them would always be closer. She let her eyes slide back to the boy she loved. "We came to visit you that one year. He took us out on his boat all day and then drove us into that little town to the movies that night. Remember that? He sat in the parking lot the whole time and waited for us. He brought a book and a flashlight. It was so cute."

Willow knew how much Vaughn had loved his grandfather. It was her house he'd walked over to the day the man had died. He'd cried and told her all sorts of stories about his visits to Lake Cedar Ridge. It was the most vulnerable she'd ever seen him, and it was a moment she'd told nobody else about. Not even Cesca. It would always be just theirs.

"But, I mean ... you couldn't have found us a place like this with, I don't know...," Cory started. "Electricity? Or, you know, furniture?"

This got the whole group laughing again. "Hey," Vaughn said. "I told you to pack like this was a camping trip."

"I still don't even understand how you found this place," Cory said. He turned and pointed back to the house. "This can't be an Airbnb listing." Then he nodded to the side of the yard, where the remains of an old chicken coop sat like a relic of days gone by. "I mean, this place is so run-down even the chickens left for better accommodations."

Vaughn waved him off. "Are you done complaining?"

Cesca punched Cory in the shoulder. "Yes, he *is*. Let's get this party started, guys."

"I can't believe you actually just said that," Willow said.

"Corny, but I agree," Vaughn said, walking toward the side of the house. "Come on, Cor. Help me with the stuff. Ladies, take a load off. Enjoy the facilities."

Vaughn and Cory disappeared around the corner of the house to the sounds of Willow and Cesca's snickering.

But one girl's laugh was missing.

Willow turned and saw that Eva had wandered away from the group, much closer to the pond now. But she wasn't looking ahead to the water. Instead, she was staring into the dense forest, her head turning left and right just the tiniest bit, as if she were trying to catch sight of something that didn't want to be seen.

It reminded Willow of the way she herself had stared at the carvings surrounding the living room entryway.

8

Willow found herself walking toward Eva before she fully understood what she was doing. The grass crunched under her feet, the taller blades reaching up to scrape across her ankles, and she must have been moving fast, because from behind her Cesca's voice called out, "Willow?" and Willow heard the apprehension, the concern.

Either Cesca's shout or the sound of Willow approaching her caused Eva to spin around on her heel, her face dominated by the same look she'd had earlier with Vaughn, the one right before she'd switched on her smile. The one that looked worried. Only this time, the smile didn't flash. Eva's face remained stone, her eyes looking very much full of some deeper wisdom as she stared directly into Willow's own gaze.

It wasn't until Cesca jogged up and stopped beside Willow that Eva's face returned to normal, looked more relaxed.

"What were you looking at?" Cesca asked. "See a deer or something? Do deer come out when it's this hot? I don't even know."

Eva looked from one girl to the other. Shrugged. "I'm not really sure," she said, her voice light and airy and trying too hard to sound casual, Willow thought. "I just thought I saw something ... moving."

"You're a long way from the big city, huh?" Willow said. "Probably not a lot of wildlife visible from Daddy's penthouse, right?"

Eva's eyes widened, another quick flash of emotion, and just as Cesca was asking, "*What?*" Eva looked over the girls' shoulders and Willow heard the van's engine protesting against the heat as it emerged from around the side of the house.

Cory was behind the wheel and drove the Previa toward the pond, swooping around in a U and then backing up like he was about to unload a boat into the water, stopping ten yards or so short of the edge. He parked, jumped out, and then jogged clumsily toward them, stripping off his shirt to reveal his white, thin torso, shouting, "You could cook a frozen pizza in that van right now!"

"Jesus, Cory," Cesca laughed. "Has your chest seen the sun this decade?"

"I plead the Fifth," Cory said, passing them and motioning them to follow him back inside the house. "Come on, Vaughn and I took the bags upstairs to the bedrooms. He's changing into his trunks."

The girls headed inside, and when Willow felt the hairs on the back of her neck begin to prickle, she looked over her shoulder and saw Eva staring daggers back at her. Maybe it was just because they'd stepped back inside the cool sanctuary of the house, but Willow shivered a chill. Nobody spoke until they'd reached the top of creaky stairs, when Cory started giving directions.

"I'm here," he said, pointing to the first door on their left. "The VIP suite." Willow glanced inside and saw Cory's green sleeping bag on the floor next to his backpack, where he'd apparently stuffed all the belongings he needed for their trip. "Willow and Cesca are the next room up on the left," Cory added. "You can tip me later for carrying the bags up. And, Eva, you and Vaughn are up there on the right. Now, if you'll excuse me, I'm going to change. If you think my chest is white, well..."

All three girls' laughter echoed down the hallway as they made their way to their rooms. Willow and Cesca entered theirs and shut the door just as Eva knocked on her and Vaughn's closed door and said, "Are you decent? I sure hope not!" and then went in.

"Ugh." Willow couldn't help from showing her disgust. When she turned around, Cesca was standing in the middle of the room with her arms crossed and a stern look on her face. Willow knew this look, knew a lecture was coming. "What is it?" she asked, rolling her eyes. "What have I done?"

Cesca shook her head. "You know exactly what you've done. What you're *doing*. You're being a one hundred percent grade A bitch to Eva."

Willow grinned. "Guess I wasn't subtle enough about it, huh?"

Cesca took a step back, looked Willow up and down with a furrowed brow. "Jesus, what's gotten into you? Ever since we got here you've been like ... like..." She blew out a breath and shrugged. "You're not acting like the Willow I know."

"You know I don't like her. And you know why."

"Oh, grow up, Willow!"

Cesca's voice filled the room with a presence neither of them had expected, and they both stared at each other, the weight of this potential argument forming above them, ready to crash down if they'd let it. They'd been best friends for so long now, and throughout that time they'd only managed the occasional small squabble or disagreement. This fight, though, this moment brewing between them, felt different. Bigger.

"Grow up?" Willow asked.

"Yes. Grow the fuck up. I get it ... you're in love with Vaughn. We all know it, Willow. Hell, even Vaughn probably knows it by now. But he's with *Eva*. And whether they last another week or another lifetime, it doesn't matter because right here, right now, he's with her. And she's done nothing wrong but manage to have a nice and handsome guy ask her out and become her boyfriend. She's been nice to us from the beginning, has never tried to overstep, and has never once—

at least that we know of—gotten jealous or given Vaughn shit when he hangs out with just us. And, yeah, she's gorgeous, okay, I can admit that. That alone is probably enough to piss off other girls, but again ... that's not her fucking fault." Cesca took a breath. Held it and then let it out. "And, hey, maybe they break up, right? Maybe down the road they split and you can get your chance to tell Vaughn how you feel. Then maybe things work out, maybe they don't, but the truth is you've had *years* to tell Vaughn you love him and you never did. So as far as I'm concerned, you—" She paused, then decided to go ahead and leap. "You have nobody to blame for your melodramatic misery except yourself."

The room fell silent but at the same time seemed to buzz with a hot electricity that caused sparks to fly inside Willow: anger and betrayal and what was that other thing she could feel waking up in her heart ... *vengeance.*

Cesca was still standing in the middle of the empty bedroom, the big window behind her with the view of the front yard and the trees and those mountains framing her perfectly and—

And Willow sees herself moving, watches in her mind as the scene unfolds in slow motion. She could unleash these fiery emotions all at once and show Cesca just how wrong she was about everything, how wrong she was not to choose Willow's side. Willow sees in her mind's eye as she rushes forward and tackles her friend, pushing her backward, slamming her into the big window. The glass would explode outward, and with it, her momentum causing her to fold over backward and flip through the air, Cesca would fall to the ground below, able to stare back up into Willow's grinning face all the way until she slammed into the earth and the world would go permanently dark. Willow could practically hear the sound Cesca's neck would make when it snapped.

"To make matters worse," Cesca said, her voice bringing Willow's mind back to the bedroom that was still based in reality and not her rage-induced fantasy, "you're so fixated on what you think you want, you don't even see what's right in front of you. What you could have if you ever stopped and got real for a second or two."

Willow's face must have said it all, because as she just stared dumbly at her friend, now it was Cesca's turn to roll her eyes. "*Cory*, you idiot. Cory is head over heels for you. And come on, you two would be perfect together. I've thought that ever since high school, Willow. I mean, you guys have the same sense of humor, you nerd out over your movies and all the geeky shit. And, hey, he's cute, right? Even if he *is* the color of the Pillsbury Doughboy."

Cesca smiled. Just a little, but enough to let Willow know that her friend was trying to take hold of the wheel and steer them back onto a smoother surface. And for a moment, Willow thought she would let her. Let things calm down and go back to normal. But ... there was that buzz of energy still there, weaker, but still present, like a pot of water that had reached a boil and then been taken off the burner, the bubbles calming but the water still dangerous to touch.

And with the energy came a new thought, one that Willow was disappointed for not having figured out before. "You want him for yourself, don't you?" she said.

Cesca laughed. "Cory? Uh, no. Like I said, he's perfect for *you*." She looked away, a quick glance toward the window.

Willow caught something in that glance but ignored it, shook her head. "Vaughn. You want him for yourself, which is why you're giving me such a hard time and now trying to pawn me off on Cory."

This is it, Willow thought. *This is where she'll get really angry. This is where the truth really comes out and we'll—*

The image of Cesca falling from the broken window was back now, replaying at the front of Willow's mind.

But instead of getting angry, instead of lashing out and yelling or telling Willow how ridiculous she was being, Cesca took a slow step forward, her eyes suddenly full of a soft sympathy that temporarily worked to calm that buzzing inside of Willow. She reached out and took both of Willow's hands in hers, her skin soft to the touch, the heat of their friendship burning between them, melting away the tension. "Willow, what's wrong? What's really going on with you? This isn't ... this is *not* you."

Before Willow could answer, from the hallway came the sound of Vaughn and Eva coming out of their bedroom, calling for everyone to hurry up and come join them. Cory hollered something back that caused Eva to laugh, and there were footfalls on the rickety stairs that eventually faded away, leaving the two girls once again in silence.

Cesca looked deep into Willow's eyes for several seconds before finally letting go of her hands and stepping back. "Come on," she said. "Let's get changed. We're here to have fun, remember?" She stepped over to her suitcase and unzipped it, flipping open the lid and saying, "Oh, I almost forgot." She reached in and pulled out a bottle of pineapple rum, set it on the floor. "Should we take a shot before heading out?"

Willow suddenly found that she wanted more than just a shot. She wanted the whole bottle.

"Sure," she said. "Like you said, let's get this party started."

They shared a laugh, and then they each took a swig before Cesca screwed the cap back on the bottle and set it in the corner of the room next to her suitcase.

9

As they walked down the steps, cobwebs waving to them from the ceiling corner, towels wrapped around their swimsuit-clad bodies, Cesca asked Willow, "What was that quip about Eva and her daddy's penthouse all about?"

Willow decided to tell her friend the truth, to try and make amends for her lashing out in the bedroom.

What was all that about, anyway? Willow wondered. She'd gotten so angry at Cesca, so ... *fuck, I was definitely irrational.* She loved Cesca, loved all of them except for Eva. Eva was her only enemy here this weekend, so why was she trying to pick fights with her best friend? Willow had woken up that morning excited and nervous, butterflies in her stomach as they'd all piled into Vaughn's van. And yeah, she didn't like Eva, the mere sight of the girl made her skin crawl, but she'd certainly not felt this ... angry. This *hostile*. It was like storm clouds full of thunder and lightning had distorted her thoughts, ever since...

Ever since we got to this house.

Willow actually smiled at this thought, wished she could share it with Cory. Because *that* was a definite horror movie trope. The haunted house that preys on its occupants and makes them do crazy things. Makes them lose their minds. *The Shining*, anyone?

"Willow? Hello?"

Cesca had stopped on the bottom step and turned around to look up at Willow, eyebrows raised, waiting.

Willow continued down, stepping around her and peering around the wall and down the hallway to make sure they were alone. Then she leaned in close to Cesca in that conspiratorial way they'd done since they were children and said, "She's not who she says she is."

"Who? Eva?"

Willow nodded. "Yes."

Cesca shrugged her shoulders (which sparked another flame of irritation inside Willow that she quickly tried to extinguish) and said, "She hasn't really told us much."

"Bingo," Willow said. "She told Vaughn she was from upstate New York, remember?"

"Yeah, sure. Some small town."

"Small town … right." Willow was smiling now, because it felt good to expose Eva for the liar she was, even if she knew it would do no real good telling Cesca, because for all the great qualities Cesca possessed as a best friend, her ability to keep a secret, no matter how juicy, was undisputed. "Would you like to guess the average home sale price of said small town? I looked it up."

Cesca just stared.

"Eight point three million dollars, Cesca. It's a fucking haven for the rich. A bunch of mansions squirreled away a few hours from the big city. I dug a little deeper and found out that Eva's dad is the president of a big advertising agency in New York City and is also currently serving on the board of two big tech companies. Eva's family is *loaded*, Cesca."

Cesca stared some more, for longer than Willow liked. Finally, she said, "Why do you know all of this?"

Willow grinned. "I need to know my competition. Keep your enemies closer and all that. The point is, Eva has never talked about any of this to Vaughn or us. She's lying, acting like she's just another normal college kid, when in reality she could probably pay all our tuitions with her monthly allowance."

Cesca cleared her throat. Looked around the foyer and then let her eyes linger on the ugly green couch in the living room. Looked back to Willow and said, "I mean, can you really blame her? Would you really want to go around school being known as the rich girl? Think about all the assumptions people would make about you. I mean, hell, Willow, look how you're acting about her right now. You think she'd want the whole school to act that way? Can you imagine trying to decide if every person who was nice to you was being genuine or if it was just because they knew you were rich?"

Willow shook her head. "You're missing the point."

Cesca put her hands on her hips. "And what's that?"

"She *lied* to Vaughn."

"Willow, did you ever stop to think that maybe she told Vaughn, that she was honest with him and trusted him with her secret and he's being respectful of that? That maybe he's known all along but wants *us* to treat her normally? Wants us to like her for her? Which I know is difficult for you, because of your situation, but maybe you should stop *only* living in that fantasy of yours and realize that Vaughn might have a life that doesn't necessarily include you or take you into account for every little thing he does."

That buzz in the air again, that tingle of electricity sparking the fuse to the powder keg buried inside of Willow. She could hear the thunder, smell the storm coming. She clenched her fists, squeezed them tight. Wanted to shout obscenities and hurl insults and...

And she's right, Willow knew. As much as she hated it, Willow understood that Cesca was absolutely correct. It didn't change how Willow felt about Vaughn, however, and it only made her realize she needed to act fast, before the part of Vaughn's life that didn't include her continued to grow bigger and bigger until one day he'd wake up and not think about her at all.

"Are you okay?" Cesca asked. "Need another shot before we go out?" She grinned, and Willow couldn't help but grin back. This was what true friendship was. The ability to tell it to each other straight, no matter if feelings might get hurt, and then turn right around and act like nothing had happened at all.

"No," Willow said. "I'm okay." She stepped close and gave Cesca a hug. "Thank you."

They walked down the hall and into the kitchen to head out to the pond. This time, when Willow smelled freshly brewed coffee, the aroma so strong she could practically taste it, she kept it to herself.

10

The shriek that pierced the air caused Willow and Cesca to stop in their tracks only a few feet from the house's back door. Their bodies tensed in unison, eyes scanning ahead of them, searching for the source of the noise, and in that split millisecond that Willow's brain was processing everything, the shriek changed, morphing away from fear and becoming gleeful laughter. The laugh was followed by a big splash, and Willow raised her hand against the sun as her eyes adjusted and she saw Vaughn standing shirtless in just his swim trunks on the dock, laughing while Eva dog-paddled toward him and then splashed him from the water.

"Oh, I'm totally getting you back for that!" Eva yelled, splashing him again.

"Only if you can catch me!" Vaughn called back as he bounded down the dock and then did a cannonball off the end.

Eva swam closer to the shore and then used the dock to pull herself up from the water, the sun glistening off her wet, perfect body, and Willow was glad that it was actually Cesca who said, "Okay, maybe I do hate her a little. That looked like something out of the *Sports Illustrated* swimsuit issue."

Willow knew Cesca was only joking, but the moment still felt good. Stepping out of the *house* felt good, as if the sunlight was doing more than just warming Willow's body, was also helping her to slough off the storm-cloud mood she'd been feeling inside. She needed to reset, try and recalibrate. She might have nothing but distaste for Eva, but the rest of them were her favorite people on earth, and this was supposed to be a fun, relaxing holiday weekend. How many more opportunities like this were they going to get together? Time was going by faster than ever, it seemed, and Willow knew that she was only a few blinks away from waking up and realizing that college was over and the real world would be waiting.

"Race you to the water," Willow said and then took off in a sprint, her bare feet a blur in the grass, grabbing her towel as it came loose and letting it fly out behind her like a cape. In those seconds as Willow ran, the sun at her back, the water calm and inviting ahead of her, begging her to jump in, she felt completely free. She felt weightless.

We're going to have the best time this weekend, she told herself, a big and honest smile breaking out across her face.

And they did ... for a little while.

11

For an hour or so, the day felt very normal for a bunch of college-aged kids hanging out on a hot day by a body of water. The hatch of the Previa was open and the cooler sat inside, full of drinks that were mostly of the alcoholic variety. They took turns syncing their phones to the big Bluetooth speaker Cesca had brought and subjected the group to their favorite playlists, and while the music blasted they all sipped their drinks and lay out on the dock and splashed around in the water for a bit. Willow and Cesca hopped in the rowboat and started making a small lap around the perimeter of the pond while Vaughn and Cory and Eva tossed a football around, but as they got further away from the group and closer to the tree line, Willow was grateful that Cesca said she wanted to turn back because her arms were getting tired.

As they rowed into the shadows the trees cast across the water, Willow felt an uncomfortable coldness begin to grow inside her that was more than just the coolness from the shade. It made her feel lonely, and worse ... *heartless*. It made her feel empty.

She quickly agreed with Cesca and they propelled themselves back to the dock.

"Did you feel that?" Willow asked as Cesca secured the boat.

"Feel what?"

"Over by the trees. It was cold."

Cesca scoffed. "Cold?" she said, pointing up to the sky, where the sun was still burning hot but also beginning its slow descent for the evening. "Are you kidding?"

Willow shrugged. "Guess I just had a chill or something."

"I hope you're not getting sick. I know there was something going around the dorms last week. My suitemate got it. Knocked her out for a day or so." Then Cesca glanced over Willow's shoulder, nodded and said, "Speaking of knocked out ... hold on."

"Wha—"

Willow heard the rapid footfalls on the wooden dock just a second before a set of arms wrapped around her belly and pulled her to the left, tossing her into the pond. The water was warm but still shocked her, and she sputtered and kicked and broke the surface and looked through blurred eyes just in time to a smiling Cory jump in after her.

"You turd," she said, laughing.

"Not your best insult," Cory said, treading water and motioning for her to follow him as he paddled toward the shore, near the van where Vaughn and Eva were standing and watching. "Come on." When he got to where the water was shallow enough that he could stand with just his chest and shoulders above the water, he called for Vaughn and Eva to come in. "Willow and I hereby challenge the golden couple to the highly sophisticated and greatly competitive game known as Chicken. Dost thou accept?"

Vaughn looked at Eva, Eva nodded, that bright smile of hers outshining the sun, and then Vaughn placed a hand over his heart and said with bravado, "Challenge accepted."

Willow cycled through emotions, her thoughts spinning through scenarios like a roulette wheel. Part of her was thinking back to what Cesca had said to her inside the house, about how Cory had a major crush on her. This was probably his attempt at flirting—maybe the first major attempt he'd ever really gone for, since things had always been so platonic between the two of them—and he was looking forward to having his head between her legs. Willow didn't want to give him the wrong idea by agreeing to his game. Plus, even though she was wearing a very modest one-piece swimsuit, the idea of being put up in the air and on display directly across from Eva and her Egyptian goddess body made Willow want to drown.

There's more to me than just my body, Willow worked to convince herself, knowing damn good and well it was true.

Vaughn likes me for me—he always has. Thinking these thoughts was one thing. Standing up for them was something entirely different.

What did make the biggest impact on her decision, however, had nothing to do with her body or with Cory and Vaughn. It was the fact that if she agreed to the game, she could literally attack Eva. Could grab her and shove her and try to topple her from her throne. All in the name of fun.

"I've got my money on Cory and Willow," Cesca called. She'd moved to sit next to the cooler in the back of the van, her feet dangling over the edge and making her look like a small child, except for the White Claw in her hand.

"Ready?" Cory asked Willow. There was water dripping down his sunburnt face.

Willow watched as Vaughn hunched down in the water and Eva wrapped her long legs around his neck and took up her position on his shoulders.

"Ready," Willow said, putting on her game face.

More ready than you even know.

12

Willow didn't hold back. From the moment the game started, she went at Eva with the ferocity of someone fighting off an attacking bear. In the first few seconds, she leaned forward, nearly toppling Cory over, grabbed both of Eva's shoulders and shoved her with such force that Eva's head snapped back. She grunted like the air had been knocked out of her and fell backward off Vaughn's shoulders.

"*Damn*, Willow. What the hell?" Vaughn said, quickly spinning to check on Eva.

Willow felt a twinge of guilt, not because of what she'd done to Eva, but because of Vaughn's reaction—like she was suddenly the bad guy.

Thankfully—or not, depending on how you looked at things—Eva came up from the water and shook her wet hair from her face and said, "Oh, I see we're playing for real now." She had that big smile on her face while she shook Vaughn's concern away and climbed back onto his shoulders.

Once she was back into position, the smile vanished, and she looked at Willow with that stone-faced stare that Willow was beginning to think was more likely who Eva really was instead of the happy, always smiling girl.

Oh, it's on, bitch, Willow thought. And it was.

The girls lunged at each other and spent the next thirty seconds grabbing shoulders and locking fingers and twisting wrists and shoving and pulling and gritting their teeth and calling upon all the strength they had, each of them refusing to go down, desperate to defeat the other. Cory and Vaughn were laughing but both struggling to keep the girls upright, fighting the momentum, battling gravity.

Vaughn was taller, and stronger, with those broad shoulders that were basically meant to be sat upon. Cory was doing his best, but just as Willow got a particularly strong hold on Eva's shoulder and pulled, hoping to yank the girl forward and over Vaughn's head, instead the force of the pull brought *Cory* forward, and he lost his footing, stumbling into Vaughn's chest. Eva seized the moment and shoved Willow back in the opposite direction, and this time it was Willow who let out a grunt and cried out as she was suddenly looking up to the sky for just a second before she splashed down into the water.

The sky went blurry, a mirage above the surface of the water, a painting caught in a rainstorm and beginning to drip, and then disappeared completely and was replaced by the pond's murky bottom as Willow flailed her arms to spin herself over. Water rushed up her nose and she gagged and choked, seeing a stream of air bubbles parade out in front of her and make their way toward the surface, heading toward the light. Willow was sinking, she realized, still trying to get her bearings, and she felt that anger again inside her, joining with embarrassment at having Eva win the battle. She screamed with what air was left in her lungs and then tried to use her legs to piston herself up and out of the water, but...

But that was when it grabbed her.

Something hidden down by the bottom reached out and wrapped around her ankle, hard and relentless. Willow's eyes went wide with fear and her heart jolted her entire body rigid. She cried out again, but there was no air left, and the two little bubbles that escaped her mouth were desperate and sad and all the indication she needed to know that she would die soon if she couldn't break free from—

She knew what had her in its grip. That roughness that rubbed at the skin of her ankle, the piercing pain where it dug in to pull its prey in for the kill. All Willow had to do was twist her torso around, look behind her and peer through the murky water growing more distorted as the disturbed sediment floated up around her like a cocoon, and she'd see it. See one of those grotesque arms from the carving around the living room entryway. See those talons draw blood, tinting the water.

She tried to jerk free and there was more pain, and this time when she tried to scream there were no bubbles at all and her heart sounded like a drum in her ears and the water was getting darker and darker and she knew it was not the water at all, but her oxygen-starved brain shutting down.

At least I won't feel it eating me, Willow thought. *At least I'll be gone before the real pain hits.*

Hands gripped her shoulders, looped under her armpits and started to pull up. More hands on her ankle, and these were gentle hands, gentle but hurried and—

And she was free. The hands pulled her up and she imagined she was one of those bubbles rising to the surface, easy-peasy. The sunlight blasted onto her face with the most amazing warmth, and in a blink Willow found herself on her back, lying in the grass on the edge of the pond, gulping down sweet air in huge heaving gasps.

"Should we do CPR?" somebody asked.

"She's breathing, right? And her eyes are open. Doesn't that mean something?" That was Cesca.

Willow coughed and tasted pond water clinging to the back of her throat, metallic but not altogether unpleasant. Her eyes were burning, stinging as she tried to blink away the pain. She could still hear those voices around her, asking if she was okay, asking her how many fingers they were holding up. She tried to focus on them, wanted to tell them all that she was fine, but she couldn't quite get her voice to work, and her vision was still blurred. Plus … there was something else. Something felt different. Felt like even though Willow had broken free of the pond's depths and had returned to the surface, she hadn't returned to the same place she'd left behind.

It was Eva's gasp that broke through the clouds, shined a light on Willow's feeling, directed her toward the sense of that uneasiness. Willow let her head roll to the side, the grass and dirt hot on her cheek, and what she saw made her want to scream, but even though she had the air in her lungs now, the best she could conjure was a soft whimper.

Willow couldn't explain it, but the backyard appeared cut in two. Where Willow was lying with her friends huddled around her was still basking in the sunlight, but maybe twenty yards away, just behind the van, somebody had turned off the day and switched on the night. Stars that were too big and too close burned like scattered moons in the dark sky, emitting a blue haze around them as they seemed to float untethered, reminding Willow of the lava lamp her dad still had in his basement man cave. Screams shattered any illusion of tranquility the nighttime spectacle might have offered, and when Willow's gaze was drawn to the source of those nightmarish cries of suffering, what she saw finally got her own scream to escape her lips, and she jumped up onto her knees.

The old chicken coop along the edge of the yard was completely ablaze, flames leaping toward the sky to shake hands with those moon-sized stars. Willow watched as behind the mesh-wire fencing, bodies writhed and jerked and fell and rolled on the ground as their flesh melted off their bones. Willow felt her stomach roll, felt a flood of heartbreak and guilt, as she understood who those imprisoned and tormented bodies belonged to.

Cesca. Cory. Eva. Vaughn.

Willow threw up, tasted the sour bile burn her throat along with more of that metallic pond water, and as her head felt light—*bubbles*, she thought, *just like the bubbles*—and the darkness crept in again, Willow took another last look at the shape standing on the outside of the burning chicken coop.

It was her. The nightmare version of her stood and watched as her friends perished in agony. The orange glow from the flames highlighted a smile on her lips. A fire-red gas can dangled from her hand.

13

Willow opened her eyes to slits, narrow windows showing a sky that had softened as the sun was blotted out by a wall of clouds. When her eyes fully opened and she blinked away the sandpaper grit that seemed to blur her vision, she saw a semicircle of faces all staring down at her, somber and expressionless, and Willow thought that this must be a corpse's point of view from the casket at a funeral home viewing.

Have I died? she thought. *Why isn't anyone saying anything?*

And then they did.

A collective shockwave of relief reanimated the four faces staring down at her. Well ... three of them, anyway. Cesca laughed and used the back of her hands to wipe away the tears that had trickled down her cheeks, and then she collapsed onto Willow's chest and wrapped her in a hug and kissed her smack dap on the lips. "Bitch, I thought you were ... *Christ*, I'm glad you're okay. What happened?"

Cory and Vaughn gripped each other's shoulders like a pair of proud dads looking down on a child who'd just won an award or scored the winning points in a game, and Willow watched as their personalities seemed to slide back into them like a lost spirit rejoining its body. When Cory saw Willow lock eyes with him, he almost sheepishly held up a bit of broken tree branch that looked covered in brownish-green slime. "I think the pond won the game," he said. "Your foot somehow got snagged on this big tree limb that was half-buried in the muck down there. I—"

"Cory was a fucking boss man and dove down and set you free and we pulled you up," Vaughn jumped in. "Then ... well, we don't know what happened. We were all ready to go paramedic on your ass, but you started moving again, and you were breathing, and—"

"And your eyes were open," Cesca said. "But it was weird, Willow. It was like you could see, but you weren't really looking at anything."

"I think she was in shock or something," Cory said.

Vaughn nodded. "Yeah, maybe shock. We thought you were okay and everything, but then you, like, I don't know, it was like you just jerked up onto your knees and you got this real scared look on your face. We started calling your name, asking you what was up, but you didn't even glance at us." Vaughn took a big breath and shrugged. "Then you threw up and passed out and here we are."

Cesca held out her hand and Willow took it, allowed

herself to be gently pulled to a sitting position. "You were only out like thirty seconds or so, but it was long enough for us to freak the fuck out." Cesca sat down next to Willow and put her arm around her. "Are you okay? Do you want something to drink? Something to eat?"

Cesca's skin was warm across Willow's shoulders, and Willow leaned in close, trying to absorb the heat, feeling like her insides were frozen solid with...

Grief, Willow thought. *And guilt. I killed you. I burned you all alive.*

"Hey, babe, it's okay. She's fine," Vaughn said, and Willow looked up just in time to see the guy she loved wrap Eva in a tight hug and kiss her forehead. "It was a complete accident," he said. "It wasn't your fault."

Eva hadn't spoken a word since Willow had come to. Hadn't moved, as far as Willow knew. And when Vaughn released Eva from his hug and stepped away, Willow found the girl staring directly at her, that now-familiar blank look on her face, as if trying to see *through* Willow, find the truth on the other side.

Willow remembered the gasp she'd heard as she'd lain on the grass after Cory and Vaughn had pulled her from the pond—*Eva's* gasp—and how the sound had been accompanied by the horror-filled vision of her friends' demise. She remembered the other times today that Eva had seemed to have fallen into this same trance, staring at nothing, stockstill, remembered the moment they'd all arrived at the house and Eva had been lost to them for a moment, only to return with her unlikely story of seeing people in the windows.

Willow had no understanding of what had happened

after she'd been pulled from the pond; the what and why and the how all were out of her reach. But Eva's gasp and the look on her face now did give Willow one thing for certain. Whatever Willow had experienced, whatever she'd seen, Eva had experienced it too.

And she's afraid of me, Willow thought. *She thinks I'm going to kill them all.*

14

Willow joined Cesca inside the opened hatch of the van, their feet dangling off the edge and waiting for the monster to grab them. Cesca had offered Willow a bottle of water from the cooler, and Willow had swished a swig around in her mouth and spat and then quickly downed the entire thing. When she reached her hand into the ice in search of something stronger, she caught Cesca eyeing her, about to play mom and suggest maybe Willow stay away from the alcohol for a little bit, at least until she was sure she was completely okay after her ... whatever had happened, but in the end they arrived at an unspoken compromise. Cesca kept her mouth shut, and Willow swallowed down the urge to pop the tab on the White Claw and chug the entire thing, instead opting to take a slow, timid sip, as if *she* were the one judging whether she should be drinking, and then the two girls fell into a comfortable silence beside each other in the back of the van.

Cory, who'd walked down the dock with Vaughn and Eva before apparently feeling a tad too much like a third wheel as the sun started to dip behind the trees, painting the sky with romantic oranges and reds as Vaughn and Eva slipped gracefully into the water and seemed to effortlessly float in each other's arms, made the lonely walk back to the van with the vibrant sky at his back and leaned against the taillight.

Nobody spoke. The three of them stared ahead at the serene picture, watching the two lovebirds in the water, and though there was no real way for Willow to know what was running through her two friends' minds, in that moment she hoped they were all thinking the same thing: *Why her, Vaughn? She's not the one.*

It didn't even matter to Willow if Cory and Cesca were having this thought because they hoped Vaughn would see that his true love, *her*, had been right in front of him all this time. All that mattered was that her friends would stand together with her in her hatred for the fraud of a girl currently nuzzled into Vaughn's chest as birds chirped an evening song and the water was a ripple of colors as the sky looked itself in the mirror.

Something that sounded like a large branch cracking in the woods to their left caused all three of them to turn that direction, peer into the darkening trees.

"Probably a bear," Cory finally said, breaking the silence. "And I bet he's hungry."

He turned to face them and when Cesca saw the smirk on his face she flailed a leg out to kick him. "Shut up, Cor. But speaking of hungry..."

He nodded and reached for the cooler. "Yeah, I say it's getting to be about supper time."

"Ugh, I hate the word *supper*," Cesca said, tipping her

bottle up and downing the rest of it. "Just say *dinner* like a normal person."

"Hey, Jesus had supper. If it's good enough for him, it's good enough for me."

"Oh, suddenly you've found religion? And, yeah, Jesus did have supper ... the *last* supper. There's no more."

Cory laughed. "That's a good point. Fine, it's time for *dinner*. Hot dogs coming up. Uh, as soon as I can get Vaughn out of the water to help with the fire."

"What, you were never a Boy Scout?"

"Are you kidding me? When I was a kid the only time I went outside was to take the trash down to the end of the driveway. Now, if they had given out badges for Xbox and horror movies, I'd be in their hall of fame."

"Vaughn!" Cesca yelled, her voice like a sonic boom across the pond, echoing around them like they were inside an arena. "Tuck your boner away and come help Cory get dinner ready. Us single folk are famished, as we haven't been suckling the sweet nectar of love all day."

Willow, who all during Cesca and Cory's banter had been staring at Vaughn and Eva in the water as they'd playfully paddled about and whispered sweet nothings to each other, finally cracked a smile at this. "You been saving that one up?" Willow asked.

Cesca shook her head. "Nope. Just another example of my instant wit."

They all shared a laugh, and Willow allowed herself to be swept up in the warmth of it, only to be doused in cold water again as Vaughn and Eva stepped out of the pond, dripping wet and silhouetted with the majestic sunset behind them.

They held hands and Eva had her other arm wrapped around Vaughn's bicep, both looking so comfortable and at ease with each other, both looking so fucking perfect in their ... coupleness that Willow thought she might puke again.

She hopped out of the van without looking either Vaughn or Eva in the eyes. "I'm going to go see if the shower works," she said. "I feel gross."

"Even if it does I doubt there will be any hot water," Vaughn called to her as she headed for the house. "You can just wash in the pond."

"Cold will be nice," Willow said and left it at that.

She heard fast footsteps in the grass behind her, and for a brief moment she fantasized that it was going to be Vaughn, ready to scoop her up in his arms and say something both tantalizing and completely cheesy, like, "Want some company in there?", but it was only Cesca, who slipped her fingers between Willow's and yelled, "You all better have dinner ready when we get back or Willow and I are stealing the van and leaving you here to fend for yourselves."

She looked at Willow and squeezed her hand and winked. Willow winked back, and together they stepped inside the house.

"*Brr*," Cesca said, wrapping her arms around herself. "It really is fucking cold in here."

Colder, Willow thought. *Colder than before.* Which made sense, right? The sun was setting and taking some of the heat with it. The old kitchen wore a shroud of shadow now, dust motes no longer dancing in sunbeams but slipping off to sleep in a gray-blue haze. When they reached the front of the house, Willow found herself casting a glance over to the wooden trim surrounding the living room entryway, and out of pure curiosity she asked, "Hey, did you check out the design carved into the wall there?"

Cesca was already on the second step, heading upstairs, but she stopped and turned to follow Willow's pointing finger. "Nope. I guess we were all too concerned with whatever the hell Eva was doing in there."

Willow couldn't tell if this was a dig at Eva for being weird, or a dig at herself for being more concerned with the house's decorative architecture than she was a human's well-being. But, and maybe it was just to humor her, since Willow had obviously had a rough go of the day, Cesca hopped off the stairs and padded barefoot across the wood to examine the carvings. Willow waited, holding her breath, fingers crossed that maybe Cesca would experience the same optical illusion—*because that's all it was, right? Just an illusion. A trick of the light*—that she had when they'd first arrived.

"It's really detailed," Cesca said flatly, as if she wasn't exactly sure what she was supposed to say, which in turn told Willow all she needed to know. Cesca turned and shrugged her shoulders. "Something specific about it?"

Willow shook her head. "No. I just thought it was interesting."

Cesca craned her head up and looked at the ceiling, and then surveyed all the space around them. "Yeah...," she said. "That's one word for this place." Then she started up the stairs again. "Come on, we're going to lose the light."

15

There was no shower, but after some gurgling and groans of protest from the pipes, the water came out from the big clawfoot tub's faucet fast and cold and clear, along with that faint metallic smell. Willow swished the water around the tub's bottom to wash away the dust and a few dead bugs, watching them swirl down the drain like a miniature water park ride, and then stepped in, using a washcloth and her body wash to do her best to feel clean again. A window just above the tub allowed the remaining sunlight to spy on her, and she hopped up on her toes and looked out to the backyard to see Vaughn and Cory walking back to the van from the left, both their arms full of sticks and small branches.

Willow let her eyes slide over to the tree line, and she shuddered a chill at the thought of stepping into the woods, disappearing out of sight. She thought about what she'd seen carved into the wooden trim again—*or did I see it?*—those long, monstrous arms tipped with razor-sharp talons, and when she snapped her neck back to the right, she was suddenly sure she'd see Vaughn and Cory writhing on the ground with long gashes in their throats and their eyes sliced from their sockets, all while the branches they'd been carrying were no longer branches at all but claw-headed snakes slithering through the grass, headed for the back door of the house.

Did we close it? Willow thought. *Did we close the door when we—*

A soft click from behind her.

Willow spun around in the tub, her feet splashing in the

water, nearly slipping and going out from under her, but a hand shot out and grabbed her wrist and pulled her forward, keeping her upright.

"Hey—"

"Shhhhh." Eva put a finger to her own lips. "It's okay," she said, releasing Willow's wrist. She reached for the towel Willow had brought with her and set on the vanity and handed it over so Willow could cover herself. "We need to talk. Alone."

16

Willow would have sworn the bathroom grew darker, Eva's unexpected presence sapping the light away, bringing the clouds, and the temperature in the room seemed to drop so fast that goose bumps prickled along Willow's arms and legs, a coldness coming from somewhere other than the icy water that was still flowing from the tub's faucet.

Willow quickly wrapped the towel around her, covering her naked body, the body she'd never exactly felt shame about until now, standing exposed in front of Eva, who even in what little remained of the sun's glow, after the hours in the car and even longer hours in the sun and the water, looked divine. Being alone with Eva for the first time, trapped in such close proximity, she could smell the girl's sweat and the remaining sweet scent of lotion she must have applied early this morning before any of them had climbed into Vaughn's van, Willow's eyes with nowhere to look except upon Eva's flesh, and there was a moment where a new and primal urge worked its way from the back of her mind, elbowing competing emotions out the way, shouldering itself to the front of Willow's thoughts and announcing itself, shouting instructions.

Lust, they called it, and powerful was its voice.

Before it arrived, Willow would have thought she'd prefer leaping from the high window in the bathroom and plummeting to a painful death to being trapped in a room with Eva, locked away with the person who stood so defiantly between her and Vaughn's everlasting future together. But now, inexplicably, as if she were no longer in control of her own gaze, her own thoughts, Willow let her eyes trace a path from Eva's bikini top, and she felt a stirring in her stomach as she imagined the strings untying themselves and the fabric falling to the floor, revealing perfect—because why wouldn't they be as perfect as the rest of her?—breasts, and then up to Eva's lips, which would be soft against her own, and taste like—

Willow literally jerked back as if shocked and shook her head, throwing Lust from side to side, beating against the walls of her mind until it lay broken and discarded on the floor. Hatred took its place, and all once again felt right. She felt strong, bold. She felt like she could move mountains. She scolded herself for temporarily letting her guard down, for being duped by Eva's beauty in much the same way she knew Vaughn had been.

It's this house, something small and nearly indiscernible spoke from some deep recess of her subconscious, as if almost afraid to be recognized. *It can do what it wants with you if you let it.*

All I want is Vaughn, Willow retorted and then stepped

out of the tub, encroaching into Eva's space. Eva took a small step backward, very small, and the girls' toes were nearly touching when Willow said, "What do you want?"

But she knew. Of course she did. Eva would have to have been either incredibly dumb or blissfully ignorant not to recognize Willow's flippant attitude toward her, the cheap shots, the cold shoulders. She must have finally put together the pieces and now, Willow knew, was the first time they'd engage in direct battle, Eva ready to take her own stand, defend her relationship with Vaughn as though it was something she could control, as though she had any power of who *Vaughn* chose to love.

"How long have you had your visions?" Eva asked.

Willow felt her mind get slapped across the face, stunned by an unexpected blow. She went blank, confusion a black fog.

"I know you've had them," Eva said. "I just want to know when it all started for you because..." She tilted her head the tiniest bit to the side and *really* looked at Willow, studying her for three excruciating seconds that made Willow want to wrap the towel around her tighter. Made her want to shrink down in size and allow herself to swirl down the drain like the carcasses of those dead bugs. "Because I've never sensed anything in you before," Eva finished.

Willow's thoughts began to sputter to life again, pulled from beneath the water and gasping for air the way Willow had been pulled from the pond.

The pond...

The nightmarish daydream Willow had fallen into where she'd stood by and watched her friends burn. The gasp she'd heard from Eva, that stone-faced look the girl had given her after.

"It's okay," Eva said. "You don't have to be afraid of it. I learned that a long time ago."

Willow said nothing. Needed more.

"I've been able to ... see things, I guess you could say, ever since I was a little girl. Things most other people can't. I can't explain it, and I don't have any control over it, but all I know is there's almost always a reason for it. At first, when I was younger, I hated myself for it, thought maybe I was crazy, or a freak because nobody ever believed me. But then the Universe helped me to understand that my visions were actually a gift, a hidden talent that made me special, made me unique, and they allowed me to help people.

"I thought I was alone, but turns out there *are* others like me out there. I don't think we all have the *same*, uh, abilities, I guess you could say, but we can"—she shrugged—"I don't know, sort of sense each other sometimes. First time it ever happened to me was with this tall high school basketball player from this little town in Virginia called Hillston. Lance, I think his name was. I was down visiting my cousin right before Christmas, and her boyfriend was on the team. The game was over and the teams were shaking hands in front of the bleachers and I just happened to look over and there he was, staring at me. And I know this sounds crazy, but in just those couple seconds I felt like I knew this random dude better than I knew anybody else in my entire life. Like we were somehow hardwired to each other. I felt this strong surge of pure happiness, just a split second, and then he smiled and nodded at me. I nodded back, and he just turned and went to the locker room, but I knew then. I knew he was like me somehow. Though to be honest, I think whatever I have ... I think he had it about a hundred times stronger."

Eva stopped and took a breath. Waited for Willow to say something. When Willow only continued to stare at her, she said, "I can't feel anything in you, Willow. Nothing at all like anything I felt that day when I saw Lance. But I *can* feel something else." She lowered her voice, just above a whisper. "Something in this place. All around us. It's heavy, Willow, and ... *evil*. When I thought I saw people in the windows earlier, the feeling was so strange, so unlike anything I'd ever experienced before, it didn't even dawn on me until after that I was having one of my *other* visions. I blurted my entire secret to the whole group before I'd even realized what I'd done." She shrugged again. "They didn't really believe me, and that's fine. I probably wouldn't either, if the shoe were on the other foot. But you *can* believe me." She paused and then leaned in closer. "And I'm worried, because I know you've seen some of the things I've seen, but if you aren't like me, like, not even a little bit, then I'm afraid that means that..."

Willow was over this entire conversation. Over the theatrics of whatever drama club performance Eva was making her suffer through. Sure, she'd had a terrible dream, some sort of waking nightmare about her friends on fire, but she'd just nearly drowned, her body had been scrambling to reboot itself, fighting off shock, or whatever. It didn't mean anything. Nothing mattered except Vaughn.

"You're afraid it means what?" Willow threw up her hands. "Spit it out."

Her words must have snapped, because Eva took a step back, crossed her arms over her chest. "I'm afraid it's coming for you, Willow. I'm afraid it *wants* you."

"What does?" Willow asked, crossing her arms to mimic Eva, rolling her eyes as if she didn't believe a word.

"I don't know," Eva said.

Willow laughed. "Okay, well, then—"

"But that doesn't mean it's not real. Listen, don't get upset. I'm trusting you with this because, well, I'm just worried about you."

Willow, absolutely overjoyed at Eva setting her up so perfectly, took another step forward to close the gap between them and then leaned in close and whispered into Eva's ear, "You should be. Now get the fuck out of my way."

Willow shouldered past Eva and ripped open the door, heading down the hall to her and Cesca's bedroom.

"I'm worried about us all," Eva called from the bathroom.

Willow ignored her, the same as she'd been trying to do all day.

17

Willow shielded her eyes against the flashlight from Cesca's cell phone, which was propped against the window to light the room.

"Sorry," Cesca said, standing from the floor and stepping in front of the beam of light, the rum bottle gripped in her hand. "It was getting too dark and too creepy for me in here." She took a swig from the bottle. "I needed light and some liquid courage." She smiled and held the bottle out. "Care to partake?"

Willow grabbed the bottle from Cesca's outstretched hand and put it to her lips. Didn't bother with a sip, went for a gulp that burned her throat. And then another, and another, and another. Her throat was on fire and her tears streamed from her eyes, and she finally pulled the bottle away from her mouth and gagged, thinking she'd vomit. Instead, she coughed, burped, and felt her stomach do a few somersaults but otherwise stay where it belonged.

The room started to spin just as Cesca ripped the bottle away from her. "Yo, what the fuck? Are you trying to kill yourself?"

Willow steadied herself, stood straight. "Maybe," she said. "What do you care?"

Cesca stepped aside as Willow stumbled by on the uneven floor and unsteady feet and started rifling through her bag for some clothes. Willow let the towel drop and started getting dressed, standing in the corner of the room and staring at the wall, which made her think of the end of *The Blair Witch Project*, which made her smile, and then laugh.

Cesca, who must have been too stunned to say anything until now, asked, "Do you think that's funny, Willow? Killing yourself? And for Christ's sake, are you really so stupid you think I wouldn't care? You're my *best friend*. Always have been. I fucking *love* you."

Willow pulled an old gray hoodie over her head and then turned around, the light from Cesca's phone tossing her shadow onto the wall, a creature stretching up onto the ceiling, waiting to pounce. "She knows," Willow said, her voice cold.

Cesca closed her eyes and took a long, slow breath. "Willow, did you hear anything I just—"

"She knows, Cesca. And now she's fucking with me."

Cesca sighed. "Who knows what? What are you talking about?"

Willow found her sneakers and tugged them on while standing, an awkward act made more tedious by the alcohol flooding her nervous system. She got them both on but then stumbled to the left and fell on her ass, her stomach feeling as though she'd gone over a dip in a roller coaster. She closed her eyes and waited for the ride to end. Burped again and said, "Eva knows I'm in love with Vaughn. And now she's making up these weird—"

"Willow, for the love of all that is holy, *get over yourself*!" Cesca's voice echoed like the room was a cavern, booming from all angles, a surround-sound effect that punched Willow in the heart. "Listen to me," she said. "And I mean it, I want you to really fucking listen to me. Vaughn is dating Eva. He's happy, Willow. Anyone can see that. So, as far as I'm concerned, if you really are truly, madly, deeply in love with him, you've got two choices. Tell him, and be prepared for the consequences—which might very well include ruining your friendship—or ... don't tell him and move the fuck on. There's, like, a billion other guys on this planet, and who knows, a lot of them just might make you happier than even Vaughn could. But you'll never fucking know because you'd rather sit around and play this *woe is me* bullshit game instead of actually trying to live your life."

And then, silence. Something broken in the air, never to be repaired. Willow sat only a few feet away from Cesca, just six or seven warped wooden boards between them, but it might as well have been a canyon for how alone Willow felt.

Alone and angry.

"Fuck you," she managed to whisper, almost not trusting her voice.

Cesca stared at her for a long time, as if waiting for the apology, a shake of the head and an admission of alcohol-induced flippancy. When none came, Cesca simply turned and left the room. Willow listened as the bathroom door opened and closed and then the pipes began to gurgle and clang in the walls.

18

Nothing was going as she'd planned it.

Willow stood alone in the bedroom, the damn light from Cesca's phone still throwing her shadow onto the wall. Willow turned away, didn't want to look at even this empty version of herself. The movement made her head swim again, the alcohol in her system mocking her, and she had to close her eyes and take a few deep breaths to keep from going down.

But in the blackness behind her closed eyelids, where she was trapped alone with her thoughts, all Willow saw was a replay of the image of her friends trapped and burning in the chicken coop—only this time they were all standing silently in a row as the flames charred and blistered their flesh, their lips pursed as if fighting back the screams, and through the engulfing flames Willow could see that they were all staring directly at her. Their eyes were knowing and accusatory.

Willow opened her eyes and saw her shadow monster on the wall move in her peripheral. "*Fuck you...,*" she whispered and then reached out and knocked Cesca's phone off the edge of the window, sending it tumbling to the floor. It landed on its back, covering the flash and erasing the light, now just a tiny dime-sized glow escaping from under it across the floorboards.

Somehow, the darkness seemed to give her strength. Willow felt herself calming down, felt her anger—anger at *all* of them!—morph into a new resolve that filled her with an unimpeded sense of confidence.

Now, she thought. Because even though in the moment she hated to admit that Cesca was right, Willow knew her time of waiting and inaction had come to an end. She could see it all so clearly now, didn't have to close her eyes to see this new movie play out in her head—not her typical horror fare but a rom-com starring her and Vaughn. She saw herself walking out the house's back door and rushing across the grass to him as he and Cory cooked dinner. He'd turn to see her at just the last second, but he'd know, right before she would leap into his arms he would understand that it was finally happening, because deep inside her Willow believed that Vaughn had always been in love with her too, and now, *finally*, they would come together and complete the puzzle that neither of them had been confident enough to try to finish.

Until now.

She'd kiss him and he'd kiss her back, hard. The rest of

the world would fall away and they would be the last two people on earth and that would be just fine because his hands would be working their way under her sweatshirt and—

Willow was moving for real now, bare feet padding across the floorboards. She threw open the bedroom door and didn't stop to let her eyes adjust to the darkness in the hallway, fumbled her way down using her hands along the wall as guides. By the time she made it to the stairs, she could see a little better, and standing on the top landing she could look down and see that the downstairs was still ever so slightly tinted grayish-blue from the final dying gasps of the sun as night took over the sky. She forced herself to slow down on the stairs, even in her frenzy smart enough to know that spraining an ankle or tumbling to the floor and snapping her neck would ruin the moment, halt the movie. The stairs creaked loudly under her toes, but it was another sound, one that reached her just as she'd stepped off the final stair and stood before the front door, that caused her to stop.

Willow turned to her right, staring into the opened mouth of the living room, that ornately carved crown molding barely visible in the dark. And Willow felt a familiar chill, a tingle that everyone gets from time to time. The sometimes unshakable feeling that they're being watched. She looked up, scanned the carved wood and followed it along its path, unable to make out the imagery but certain that in those leaves she'd see those eyeballs staring back at her, curious as to her next move.

The sound again, coming from deep in the living room, and this time Willow recognized it for what it was just as the spark of flame came to life. It was the sound of someone thumbing the wheel of a small butane lighter.

The flame caught and stayed lit, and without thinking Willow walked toward it, crossing the living room threshold, feeling those eyes in the wall shift and follow her every step. She made it two steps inside the room when she realized it was Eva holding the lighter, the girl's face flickering in and out of focus behind the dancing flame. Willow looked out the window and saw that full dark had finally arrived. There were no stars in the sky. She looked back to Eva and stared, waiting, that newfound resoluteness steeling her nerves, almost pleading for a fight.

"I can prove it," Eva said, thumb still pressed down on the lighter's button, keeping the flame alive. "I can prove what I told you is true."

"I don't care," Willow said, and she meant every word of it. Eva was dead to her, had *always* been dead to her. Now she could finally stop pretending otherwise.

Eva had changed back into the clothes she'd been wearing earlier, sparing Willow the frustration of having to stare at the girl's perfect body any longer, and she reached down with the hand not holding the lighter and pulled something from the pocket of her shorts. When she brought it close to the flame, Willow could see the object was a hundred-dollar bill.

"When we touched in the bathroom," Eva said, "I could sort of ... see into you."

Willow felt herself go cold. Colder than even the chill of the house.

"I saw everything. I could read your feelings. About Vaughn ... about me."

"You—" Willow started, but Eva cut her off.

"You think I care about money? You think I'm some stuck-up, spoiled daddy's girl who gets anything she wants? You couldn't be more wrong. Yeah, my family's rich, but I hate money. I hate what it does to people. Both the ones who have it ... and the ones who lust after it."

Eva touched the corner of the hundred-dollar bill to the lighter's flame, and when it caught and started to burn she held it in front of Willow's face and said, "I don't want it. Any of it." She turned and tossed the burning bill into the fireplace, watched it smolder.

Willow shook away her chill, looked inside her again for that strength that had felt so permanent just moments earlier. "That doesn't prove anything. You being rich isn't exactly a secret if somebody knows how to use Google, and you've probably dealt with people judging you because of it your whole life. So, right now, whatever this is"—Willow gestured toward last remains of the bill in the fireplace—"I think it's because either you're crazy, or you're jealous of Vaughn's and my friendship and worried that maybe he really does love me more than he does you. Either way, I don't see how any of it's my problem."

Willow felt better, felt *good*. Felt a new hunger growing inside her, a hunger that could only be satiated by taking what she wanted. She gave Eva her most syrupy smile and said, "See you outside."

She had turned and taken two steps when Eva said, "I know it was really you who brought us here."

Willow froze, her body shocked still. Because everything else that Eva had said she could easily dismiss, but this...

Willow had been the one who found the house, or rather, had been shown the house. She'd been online, reading a page on Reddit where college students offered suggestions for more low-key and cheap spring break travel options, and she'd gotten a private message with details on the house. The person said they had been there last year and it was a perfect off-the-grid getaway. Willow had at first meant to trash the message, thinking it was spam, but when she'd seen the picture of the pond out back and the trees and the little rowboat, she'd remembered Vaughn's grandfather's place, and how much happiness those trips had brought him. Willow had a secret Reddit user account she used when she wanted to be more anonymous and used it to forward the information to Vaughn, hoping he'd take the bait. Sure enough, the very next day he'd told them all he knew exactly where they should go. Willow had gone back to reply to the sender's initial message, meaning to thank them, but somehow the message had been deleted from her account. She thought that very odd, but in the end, it didn't really matter. She'd gotten the first part of what she wanted.

How? she thought. *How does she know that?*

"I told you," Eva said as if in answer. "And, Willow, that's what scares me the most about all this. What does this place want from you?"

Willow couldn't help herself. She turned back around. Eva had let the lighter go out, so only the vague outline of her shape was visible in the dark.

"We have to leave," Eva said. "Tell Vaughn we have to leave. He'll listen to you, right?"

The two girls stared at each other's shapes across the black sea of the living room.

Crazy. Jealous.

"Tell him yourself," Willow said.

As she left the living room and headed for the hallway, she could still feel those eyes living in the sculpted leaves watching her. Only this time she felt they were looking on approvingly.

19

The heat had dissipated now that the sun had set, but the night air felt sticky and thick, like stepping out of the cold house and into a sauna. Willow pushed up the sleeves of her sweatshirt and stormed across the backyard, found Vaughn and Cory laughing over the small campfire they'd built in front of the pond, just to the left of the van. They were still in their swim trunks and shirtless, and they were cooking hot dogs on a cast-iron griddle just over the flames. By the time she'd reached them, Willow realized all the confidence she'd worked up and all the can't-stand-in-my-way attitude she'd carried with her inside the house had completely vanished. She suddenly felt very small again, nearly insignificant, like she'd somehow dropped these traits off at the door before she'd stepped out.

Maybe it was because living out a fantasy in your head was a lot safer and easier to swallow than making it a reality, or maybe it was because...

Because of the house, Willow thought but then shook her head, thinking it sounded ridiculous.

But does it?

The way Vaughn and Cory were standing on the other side of the fire from her, with the orange and yellow flickers of light lashing across their torsos, caused Willow's mind to once again flash back to the image of the chicken-coop prison inferno. The sound of the house's back door getting slammed shut snapped the image away, and Vaughn and Cory both looked up and saw Willow for the first time, and then looked past her to whoever was approaching.

Vaughn's face lit up, and not because of the flames. For a split second, Willow felt giddy excitement thinking that his happiness was because of her, but it was quickly squashed when Vaughn said, "Hey, babe, I told Cory you were good for three, maybe four hot dogs, but he didn't believe me. Says you're a one-and-done gal, for sure."

Willow didn't dare turn around, but soon there was the sound of footsteps through the grass behind her, and Eva said, "Cory, Cory, Cory … you should know better than to judge a book by its cover."

Cory punched Vaughn's shoulder, which ended up knocking *him* backward more than it affected Vaughn's stance, but Vaughn laughed and fell into feigned distress, rubbing his arm and exclaiming, "Hey, you're gonna bruise my good arm!"

Cory punched him again for good measure and said to Eva, "Hey, it was a compliment, okay? I just didn't think someone like you would down multiple dogs." Then his eyes went wide and his mouth plopped shut, realizing what he'd just said.

Eva was beside Willow now, so close her elbow brushed Willow's own, which made Willow's stomach roll and caused her to take a step sideways to add more space between them. Eva held up her hands and pretended to be offended. "Ohhhh, somebody *like me*, huh? And what exactly does *that* mean, Cory? Do tell."

Despite the glow of the fire, Willow saw Cory's face turn red. He fumbled through saying, "Uh, it's just you're so ... I mean..." In apparent desperation, he looked over to Willow, as if she might bail him out.

Not a chance, Willow thought, keeping her face completely passive.

"Sexy!" Vaughn yelled into the night. "He thinks you're one fine thang!"

Cory rolled his eyes and groaned. Let out a long, exasperated sigh and looked apologetically at Eva. Shrugged.

"I'm just messing around, Cory. Relax," Eva said. She walked forward, toeing up to the small rocks Vaughn and Cory must have found near the edge of the pond to create a border around the fire. "But seriously, you're cooking me at least two, right? I'm starving."

"Me too." Cesca's voice slapped Willow in the back, and then she stepped past without so much as a glance in Willow's direction. She'd matched Willow in style, wearing a baggy sweatshirt that fell nearly to her knees. Her hair was wet and hanging heavily down her back, and Willow shivered at thinking of washing her hair in the cold water that had come from the tub in the upstairs bathroom. It would be like dunking your head in a bucket of ice water.

Eva sidled up next to Vaughn, and he wrapped his arm around her and kissed her forehead. "Only a few more minutes, right, Chef?" he said, nodding to Cory.

"You bet," Cory said, using a pair of long metal tongs to roll the hot dogs over to char a bit more on their other side.

Cesca pointed to the tongs and said, "So *that's* what's been in your swim trunks all day. Here I was just thinking you were excited about all the half-naked girls around you."

Cory didn't look up from the fire but said, "The tongs were packed in the van all day." Then, after a beat, "Think about that..."

The group erupted in laughter. Vaughn high-fived Cory, who was grinning big, and Eva and Cesca made a show of suddenly showing extreme interest in Cory's nether regions, which caused Cory to cover himself and say, "Hey, eyes up here, ladies! I'm a human being, not an object!"

The rolls of laughter continued, echoing across the pond.

Willow never cracked a smile. And what was worse, nobody even seemed to notice or care.

20

Things had settled down, the energy of the whole group having dropped several degrees, the long, tiring day and the alcohol having caused a somewhat somber vibe to fall over them all as the night sky had rolled in. Vaughn and Cory ate their hot dogs standing up, pacing back and forth around the small fire while they chewed and talked, kicking rocks into the pond and pointing at things in the distance like explorers fascinated by a new planet. They were in their own little world, two guys just being guys—friends being friends.

Cesca and Eva were having their own moment, seated side by side in the two beach chairs that Vaughn had pulled from the back of the Previa and set up while the girls had been inside. Willow leaned against the back bumper of the van and had only taken a single bite of her hot dog before setting it at her side. She stared at her best friend as Cesca leaned in so close to Eva as she chatted that the girls' heads were nearly touching. They were both sitting identically, with their legs crossed and the paper plates with their hot dogs settled into their laps. True to her word, Eva had already demolished her first dog and was halfway through her second and Willow found that she could actually hate the girl even more than she already had. Willow kept staring, not really listening to a word that Eva or Cesca was saying but watching their faces, studying the way Cesca was throwing her head back in laughter at something Eva had said, wondering how long both of them could keep up the charade of pretending Willow wasn't there.

The boys were being boys, the girls were being girls, and Willow sat alone with an uneaten hot dog for her only friend and a sick feeling in her gut—a feeling of loneliness and loss and failure. She felt empty ... yet also full. Full of despair. Full of a sudden urge to just stand from the back of the van and walk forward, plunge into the pond and swim to the bottom and find a new branch to twist herself around and stay there until her lungs screamed for more air but no air would come and her vision would start to go dark and then everything would be finished.

She wondered how long it would take for any of them to realize she was gone.

How did this all happen? The question paraded through her thoughts again. Willow, who had played out several different scenarios for today, would never have guessed when they'd arrived at the house that by nightfall she would have managed to somehow completely isolate herself from her friends, push them away until she was nothing but an insect buzzing around their periphery—tolerated but still a nuisance, a thing you tried to ignore.

Stop!

Willow shook her head, cleared away the clouds. She was being melodramatic. Sure, she and Cesca had gotten into a big fight, but Cesca had had it coming—how *dare* she take Eva's side in any of this, even a little bit? Willow was the one Cesca was supposed to be rooting for, helping to build up her confidence to make her move, not chastise and *blame* her for her feelings about Vaughn. Hell, it wasn't Willow's fault, after all. You can't help who you love, right?

And Eva ... well, *fuck* her. Her and her money and her looks and her, *please*, psychic-ghost-seeing fuckery. Fuck it all and fuck her twice.

But, Willow realized, Vaughn and Cory were both still in her camp, as far as she knew. Both of them were oblivious to what had happened inside the house, and Vaughn had asked her if she still liked only mustard on her hot dog—*he remembered*—before he'd prepared one for her and handed over her plate with a wink and a smile that had made her heart flutter. And Cory ... well, Cesca thought he had a thing for Willow, and looking back at things, Willow thought she could see it. Allowed herself to briefly entertain the idea of what it might be like to date him. After a quick analysis, she came to the conclusion that being involved romantically was something that, if the situation was different, she might actually give a shot.

But this wasn't a different situation. The current—and *only*—situation was Vaughn.

Willow was about to stand up and go join the two boys when Eva said, "Oh, I'm taking that now. It's actually pretty interesting."

"Ugh," Cesca droned. "Forgive me if I don't believe you." (*That makes two of us*, Willow thought.) "I read enough boring old novels in high school English. I can't imagine a class called 'Contemporary Literature: An Exploration of Theme' could possibly include anything I'd call interesting. I don't even understand why I have to take it, I'm a *biology* major."

Eva laughed and stood up from her beach chair, popping the last bit of her hot dog into her mouth. She chewed twice and swallowed, said, "All freshmen have to take it. But, no, seriously, the assignments really are good reads. Like the one I'm reading now. Here, it's in the van." Eva walked up to the Previa's passenger door and pulled it open, still not even casting a side-eye in Willow's direction, and pulled a paperback book from the storage slot on the inside of the door. She tossed it to Cesca, who caught it ungracefully, her hot dog nearly rolling off her plate in her lap. "I was going to try and read a few pages on the drive up, but I started to get carsick," Eva said.

Cesca held the book up, leaning into the firelight to see better, and read from the cover. "*A Family History of Skulls*: A novel by Declan Scheider." She fanned through the pages. "I don't know, the title sounds sorta—"

"Oh my God, that's him!" Eva thrust her hand out, pointing to the back of the novel in Cesca's hands. Cesca jumped at the shout and the book tumbled from her grip, likely destined to become more fuel for their campfire if she hadn't caught it against her knee at the last second.

"What?" Cesca said. "Who are—"

She didn't get to finish because Eva had rushed over to her and snatched the paperback away. Eva leaned down close to the fire and—

I should push her in, Willow thought. *Let's see how pretty she is after she burns.*

—tilted the book just right so she could get a better look at the back cover. She nodded, stood and said, "Yep. That's totally him." She held the book up for Cesca to see and tapped the back repeatedly with her index finger as she spoke. "That's the guy I saw earlier. The one who was looking out from the upstairs window when..." She trailed off, her voice growing quieter as she must have realized what she was saying, how it must sound to everyone else. "When we first got here." Then, sounding as though she was trying to somehow defend herself, she added, "I knew I had seen him before ... somewhere."

Only then did she cast her first glance at Willow since they'd had their moment in front of the fireplace, a look that wasn't asking for help, wasn't pleading, but serving as a reminder that the two of them were the only ones privy to some greater truth that shrouded their group.

Nope, Willow thought. *Don't try and pull me into your little psycho-fantasy bullshit. You're on your own, bitch.*

It was then that Willow realized the rest of her friends had grown silent. Cesca wasn't looking at the back of the book, where Eva's finger was still pointing, frozen as if to help make her point, but instead letting her gaze move slowly back and forth between Eva's face and Vaughn and Cory. The boys were standing a few feet apart from each other by the water's edge. Cory's face was impassive, calmly waiting to see if any more would be said. Vaughn had his hands on his hips, his brow creased like he was trying to work out a puzzle while he stared at Eva.

Willow smirked. *He's trying to figure out if she's being serious. He's wondering if his girlfriend might actually be fit for the asylum. He's wondering what else about her he doesn't know yet, what other dark secrets she might be keeping.*

The silence remained, the only sounds left those of the flames licking at the kindling and the soft lapping of the pond against the shore, and Willow understood what this moment was.

It was *hers*. Eva was down, and now Willow would make sure she never got up again, would step on her throat until her and Vaughn's relationship was dead for good.

"You know," Willow said, taking a few steps to stand in front of Eva and Cesca, "you would think with all of Daddy's money, you could afford a good therapist."

The silence somehow grew louder. Everyone froze. All

eyes locked onto Willow as she stood inches from Eva, and Willow relished the feeling. Felt empowered.

"I mean, if you truly think you saw faces in the windows, and now you're positive one of them was this random author dude from your school book, well, shit, I'd say that definitely qualifies you for some grade A psychotherapy. And that's just for starters, right? What else do you think you can do, other than seeing people who aren't there, huh? Can you talk to ghosts? Communicate with aliens? Help the police with unsolved murders? Why don't you tell the group what you told me upstairs? Let everyone hear how *special* you are." Willow paused. Made a show of waiting for Eva to answer.

Eva said nothing. Remained still and quiet. But her eyes never wavered from Willow's. In fact, her eyes spoke volumes, matched the intensity of Willow's words. They gave a single, serious request.

Stop.

Willow did not stop.

"What?" Willow said. "Where'd I go wrong? Oh, let me guess. You don't really believe you can do any of those things, and you didn't see anybody out front earlier, and aside from his picture on the back of your book here you've never seen this"—she plucked the book from Eva's hands and read the name again—"Declan Scheider in your life."

In a moment of inspiration, Willow tossed the paperback into the fire. The pages caught ablaze instantly and curled at their edges, producing a plume of black smoke.

Nobody spoke. Eva still did not look away.

"So what I think," Willow said, "is that if you aren't certifiably crazy, that just means you're looking for attention.

You're a spoiled rich brat who can't stand not to have all eyes on you." Willow didn't turn, but she pointed behind her to where she knew Vaughn was still standing. "Can't stand to have your boyfriend's focus go anywhere but on you for too long or you start to feel insecure and you get whiny and pout and have to find a way to make sure people remember you're still here and you're perfect, and make sure everybody loves you, the rest of us be damned. That about right?" Willow held out her hands in front of her, palms up, signaling that she was now giving Eva the floor. "Which is it?" she asked. "Are you crazy, or just selfish? Either way, you'll never be a part of us."

There. She'd done it. Willow felt a rush of relief and pride. She felt momentarily triumphant, elated that all she'd ever wanted was about to come to fruition. Her friends would see Eva for what she really was, casting her out of their group, and Vaughn would thank Willow for showing him the truth, for allowing him to get out of what would surely become a toxic relationship before it was too late.

Footsteps coming from behind Willow broke the stunned silence, footsteps that her ears had grown attuned to over the years, that she would bet money she could pick out of a crowd. Vaughn's casual gait, slow and confident.

Here it comes, Willow beamed, preparing herself for the joy she'd be overrun with when he stopped beside her, put his arm around her and pulled her close while he questioned Eva, asked her who she really was. Asked her why she'd lied to him. Told her it was over.

But the joy never came. Instead, disbelief. Vaughn reached Willow's side and then kept moving, taking the couple extra steps to reach Eva. And he *did* put his arm around her. Wrapped her up and turned her away from the group and said, "I'm so sorry. Come on, let's take a walk."

As they moved away, headed past Cesca and toward the trees, Vaughn turned and looked over his shoulder and shot Willow a look that shattered her heart. Its message an unmistakable *What the fuck is wrong with you?*

Cesca stood from her beach chair, and Willow was embarrassed to think for a split second that her lifelong friend was coming to console her, to be the shoulder to cry on. But she should have known better. Cesca looked into Willow's eyes as though she were a stranger, then shook her head and asked, "When did you become so terrible?"

Before Willow could even attempt to answer, Cesca pushed her aside, saying, "I'm going inside. The sooner I go to bed, the sooner morning will come and we can get the fuck out of this place."

Willow turned around and watched Cesca's silhouette as it moved briskly across the grass toward the house, and her stomach sank when she saw Cory's shape jog after her. Neither of them looked back. Not a single glance.

What have I done?

Lost in her thoughts, without realizing she was moving, Willow found herself halfway down the wooden dock, making her way toward the end. When she reached the edge, toes inching out over the end of the wood, she looked down into the water.

What the fuck have I done?

21

The moonlight cast a silvery glint across the pond's surface, and in that metallic-tinted blackness Willow stared at a darkened version of herself. She could not make out her own eyes or nose or lips, but the outline of her head in the gently rippling water was unmistakably hers ... and also, oddly not her at all.

It was exactly how she felt. She was still Willow, of course she was, but her emotions had somehow usurped her normal state of being, had stormed the castle of her logic and rational thinking and now sat in the throne, in control. A ruthless leader.

This isn't me, Willow said to the featureless face looking back at her from beneath the pond's surface. *This isn't what I wanted.*

And the head beneath the water talked back. Wet, choking words filling Willow's mind.

It is ... this is ... you.

Willow felt a chill crawl from her lower back all the way up to her skull, a mouse shivering across her spine. Goose bumps prickled her arms and legs. She stepped back from the edge of the dock, taking two steps backward as the echo of that drowning voice faded from her thoughts.

"Is it?" she asked out loud.

There was no wind stirring the air, not even a gentle breeze to speak of at that moment, but a noise from across the pond drew Willow's gaze. She looked on in the darkness, hearing the familiar symphony of rustling tree limbs and branches and leaves despite the still air, seeing the crude outline of the treetops against the moonlit sky sway and shake back and forth, then jerk now and then, creating off-beat, staccato bursts of sound. Like they were trying to send a...

A message, Willow thought, feeling ridiculous but also all at once enlightened. Crazy but also suddenly seeing things more clearly than she'd ever been able to before.

New movement from her left, down near the ground. Willow flicked her eyes toward it, saw the shapes she knew to be Vaughn and Eva, walking slowly back from around the rear of the pond. Soon they'd reach the front and return to the fire, to the van, to the house.

Seeing them walk together, Vaughn's broad shoulders that Willow knew so well hunched over and in, making him look smaller as he pulled himself closer to Eva, making him look...

Weak.

The king on the throne of Willow's thoughts gave a new decree, and she found herself capitulating to it instantly. Surprised at the lack of sadness that accompanied the decision.

"I don't need you," Willow whispered across the pond.

Because maybe getting her ankle tangled in the branch and nearly drowning had been not only a near-death experience but a rebirth of some sort. An awakening of who she truly was. Maybe, and—yes, of course, she'd had it all wrong from the start. This trip—this *place*—had never been about Willow telling Vaughn how she felt but was instead about Willow discovering the person she needed to be, the person she had *always* been but had until now been too afraid and too timid to realize.

Now I'm free, Willow thought. *I'm fucking unstoppable.*

And then another whisper across the pond, a sudden truth so profound it hurt, but Willow felt pleasure in the pain.

"I don't need any of you."

Willow turned and walked back down the dock, feeling on top of the world. Feeling like life could not possibly be any better.

Everything changed when she stepped back inside the house.

22

Willow closed the back door behind her and stood just across the threshold in the old kitchen, peering into darkness as she waited for her eyes to adjust. The air was chilled, colder than ever before now that the sun had long since set, and she breathed in slow, deep breaths, letting the icy air fill her lungs. The kitchen began to take shape, the table and chairs and deep-basin sink emerging from the shadows, crawling out of hiding. The room dialed up from black to a faint gray, just enough light to see by.

Willow took another deep breath and held it. When she blew it out in a slow exhale from her lips, she found herself pulsing with a new sense of energy, her heart beating with excitement, her nerves tingling and cracking with electricity.

She moved across the kitchen floor, her body feeling strong and solid.

Confidence, she thought, realizing this new sensation for what it was.

Only as she reached the beginning of the hallway did she catch the lingering scent in the air, a faint taste on her tongue that had stowed away on one of those deep breaths.

Coffee.

The same scent she'd picked up when they'd all first stepped into the house, the one nobody but her had been able to notice. And now, as Willow moved down the hallway toward the foyer, she understood why. *It's only for me*, she thought. *This whole place ... it's all for me.*

She began to climb the stairs, and halfway up another new emotion was sent from the throne room, fiery arrows of desire raining down from the castle walls, catching the town's streets ablaze with lust.

Willow's mind went to Cory as she reached the top step with a new heat in her belly, a new tingling even lower.

He wants me, she thought. *Even Cesca said as much.*

And this is for me. It's all for me.

Vaughn was outside with Eva—and fuck 'em, let 'em have each other—and if Willow spent the night with Cory, she knew Cesca would be alone. Sit by herself in a cold, dark room while everyone else found companionship, while everyone else *fucked*, and realize that maybe she shouldn't have been so quick to take the side of a crazy, lying bitch over her best friend. Because where had that gotten her, other than being an outcast, isolated?

Sit in the corner and think about what you've done! Willow had to clap a hand over her mouth to suppress her own laughter. She stood at the end of the upstairs hallway, a black tunnel leading to the bedrooms. She imagined Cesca lying in her sleeping bag in the second bedroom on the left, wondering when Willow would return, wondering if she'd apologize, wondering if things might ever go back to the way they were before.

Keep wondering, Willow thought, stopping at the first door on the left—Cory's bedroom—and gripping the handle. She turned it gently in her hand, and the door moved surprisingly silent on its hinges as Willow eased it open enough to stick her head through the crack.

She was about to whisper Cory's name, but the word froze in her throat. The scene before her was mid-act, the dim moonlight spilling through the window and across the silhouetted figures on the floor casting the entire space into a noir shadow. Willow's heart stopped. A beat. Two. Then started again with a furious sputter. She blinked several times, her breath frozen along with her words, trying to comprehend.

Cory's sleeping bag was unzipped and spread open on the floor. He lay on his back with his arms out, his hands gripping a pair of slim thighs. Cesca's thighs.

Willow's ex–best friend was naked, straddled atop Cory's cock, and rocking gently back and forth, leaning forward with her breasts in his face and her hands planted firmly on either side of his head. They moved together in a harmony that made Willow wonder just how practiced this dance was.

Willow stared at the two people she thought she knew, her presence unknown, both the bodies on the floor too enthralled in their own act to notice their uninvited bystander. As she stared, the fires of desire burning the town in her mind were caught by a strong wind, moving faster now. And as they ravaged buildings and destroyed fields and crops, they started to change color—the passionate reds and oranges suddenly flickering into an angry, soulless black, sending a toxic charcoal smoke into the air, poisonous and rancid.

Willow breathed in this smoke, tasted its sour bite at the back of her throat.

And she found she liked it.

As softly as she'd opened it, Willow eased the bedroom door closed again. She made her way down the stairs and into the foyer, turning right and walking into the living room, seeing the branches and leaves carved into the crown molding shimmer and dance with excitement as she passed. Even though the house was still dark, Willow found she could now move easily through it, unencumbered by her lack of vision, like she'd lived here all her life and knew every step, every inch of the place.

I was blind, Willow thought. *But now...*

She reached the fireplace, found the fire poker and gripped its handle tightly in her fist.

I see.

23

Maybe Willow didn't like this new version of herself.

Maybe she loved it.

She wasn't sure which.

But as she climbed the stairs, she was sure it was too late to stop it from taking over.

The house had made sure of that.

She belonged to it.

Always had.

Always would.

24

Willow was not gentle with the door this time.

She twisted the handle and then threw the door open, and this time the hinges *did* scream. But, no, that had been Cesca, scared and startled, twisting around, her naked torso half-painted silver by the moonlight. She fell sideways, landing on her hip and then rolling onto her ass, leaving both her and Cory exposed, *caught*.

Cory was the first one to see the fire poker dangling from Willow's side, and as Willow watched the realization replace the confusion on his face, she knew he'd seen enough slashers to understand exactly what was about to happen. She knew he was calculating just how many rules he might have broken, what choices he'd made to end up the victim of his own movie.

Willow stood over the two of them, still half-shrouded in the shadows, and she could see this new version of herself reflected in their frantic eyes. The killer's true identity revealed. The gasp from the audience.

"Willow, wait." Cory. A pointless, last-ditch effort.

He should know better, Willow thought, just as Cesca started to use her heels to push herself backward, scrambling off the opened sleeping bag and pushing herself up to stand. If Willow could have seen her own eyes, she thought she would have seen those black flames roaring across the landscape. If she could have seen her own lips, she would have seen the smirk permanently affixed there as she took two quick steps forward and raised the fire poker to her side and swung it up and across in an arc.

The hooked end caught Cesca across the face, slicing through her cheek and snapping her head to the side. She tried to scream, but the sound was muffled through her mouthful of steel. She went still for a second, then two. Eyes wide, terror-filled. Then Cesca took stock of everything, realized that the pain she was now being flooded with was because her face was hooked onto the end of a fire poker like she was a fish on the end of a fisherman's line.

Two drops of blood dripped from the trickle making its way down the black shaft of the poker and fell to the floor with a one-two plop-*plop*. Cesca tried to tilt her head down to get a look, and Willow could see her friend's mind shutting down, could see shock sending all systems into hibernation.

Not yet, Willow thought. *I want you to feel this.*

Willow yanked the fire poker toward her, and the hook ripped clean through Cesca's cheek and out the front of her mouth in a spray of blood and spit and shredded skin. Cesca got as far as sucking in a gasp of air for a scream that would never come, because for her next trick, Willow pulled the poker up and into both hands and then slammed it forward, shoving the pointed tip directly into Cesca's left eye. It met no resistance, and Willow pushed forward, shoving Cesca backward as the steel pierced her brain, the back of her head slamming against the wall. Cesca's body went limp, and Willow pulled the poker free once more, feeling warm droplets of blood pepper her face as the rag doll version of the girl she'd grown up with crumpled to a dead heap on the floor.

Willow spun around at movement from behind her, just caught sight of Cory's naked ass rounding the door frame. She heard his footsteps in the hallway, and she found herself moving with speed she had never known she possessed. She leapt into the hall just as Cory had reached the top landing of the stairs.

And that was when he made another mistake that he should have known better than to make.

He paused. Looked back for just a second. And Willow wondered if all those scary movies had taught him *anything*.

That's the problem with most people, she thought. *They're so naïve. It can never happen to them ... until it does.*

She lunged. Huge, leaping strides. Cory's eyes lit up and his legs started working again, but it was too late. Always too late. He made it down three stairs before Willow reached the top landing and in a proud moment of ingenuity and deft hand-eye coordination she tossed the fire poker out like a dart and watched as it struck Cory's ankle, where it flipped around and snagged his other foot and everything got tangled and, just like that, Cory was airborne, his weight and momentum sending him flying forward, headfirst, arms pinwheeling like a cartoon character trying to fly after jumping off a cliff.

He landed on the side of his face at the bottom of the

stairs. The sound his neck made when it snapped made Willow think of the trees as they'd spoken their message to her.

25

Willow stepped over Cory's body and thought, *What a shame.*

What a shame everyone I loved turned out to be such pieces of shit. Did I ever really know any of them? After all these years, were we nothing but strangers in disguise?

She had the fire poker, its end still slick with Cesca's blood, leaned against her shoulder as she walked, like a big league slugger strolling up to the plate just knowing he was about to hit one out, give the crowd something to cheer about. It seemed to pulse in her grip, but that might have just been her own energy, radiant and high-voltage, practically bursting from her, needing to be channeled out.

And Willow knew exactly how to fix that.

She reached the kitchen and was about to step out the back door when she caught the aroma of coffee again, stronger than ever, cloying. It pulled her head to the left, and there, on the counter, she saw it. An old tin coffee can, perfectly spotlighted by the slice of moonlight coming through the window. She moved toward it as though caught in a tractor beam, her original path diverted, and saw that the can's lid was already off. In Willow's newfound form of night vision, she would swear she saw a shimmer in the air just above the can, like it was full of not coffee but hot asphalt on a midsummer day. The scent grew so strong it was nearly overpowering, threatened to choke her.

But Willow could not pull away.

She leaned her head into that shimmer and looked inside the can and saw that the coffee grounds were twinkling in the moonlight. Without thinking, completely on autopilot now, she scooped a handful of the grounds into her palm and shoved them into her mouth. It was bitter and gritty, like a mouthful of sand, but Willow chewed and chewed and chewed and then swallowed down every last bit, licked her lips to clear away any remains.

She felt the energy inside her grow nuclear in strength. Felt all that had stubbornly remained of her old self get washed away in the rain, all traces erased. She laughed in the kitchen, her voice echoing around her in delight. When the noise faded, Willow stepped through the back door to do what she'd set out to do from the very beginning of this trip.

Show Vaughn exactly how she felt.

26

Willow moved slowly and quietly through the grass, a predator stalking its prey. The energy boiling inside her made the task difficult, because she had to fight hard against her desire to sprint, to fall upon her victims with an intense ferocity. The promise of the sweet taste of satisfaction and—yes, she'd call it *revenge*—was just enough to keep her patient. Taking care of Cesca and Cory had almost been too easy, and Willow didn't want to get cocky. Didn't want to rush and risk ruining what would be her perfect ending.

At first she didn't see Vaughn or Eva anywhere, but as Willow inched her way step by slow step toward the van and the campfire, the fire poker held down at her side, its tip tracing a line through the grass, a small bit of movement finally caught her eye. She was maybe ten yards from the front of the van, and she found them both lying on a big blanket spread out just a few feet from the water's edge. They were on their backs, staring up at the sky, firelight tossed from the campfire's flames flickering across the top half of their bodies while pale moonlight painted their legs and feet.

Willow crouched down and leaned against the van's low, sloped hood, poking her head around the side, feeling another wave of revolt as she watched Vaughn lift Eva's hand, whose fingers were intertwined in his, and press it to his lips, long, slow and soft. It was an intimate, sensual act. Something more full of love than anything Willow had ever experienced herself. The type of thing she'd fantasized about for years, to be the girl on the blanket next to Vaughn, to feel his touch, his lips against her skin.

That was what the old Willow wanted. The old Willow who gave people more chances than they deserved and thought good things would come to those who waited.

The new Willow, the Willow who had now creeped around the side of the van and stood just a few feet from the campfire, its heat too hot and unpleasant against her face, the Willow that now watched as Vaughn said something that made Eva laugh, something Willow couldn't hear because of the electricity buzzing in her ears, wanted only death.

Death to those who had caused her pain. Death to those who had rejected her.

Willow stepped around the campfire, its crackling flames hiding her footsteps. Close enough to them now that she could see the scar on top of Vaughn's head, the result of a playground accident when he was just a kid, before he'd moved to town and joined Willow on the bus that morning long ago. The hair didn't grow there now, a tiny bald sliver no longer than half an inch, maybe. Willow's eyes trained onto this perfect bull's-eye atop Vaughn's skull and she lifted the fire poker from her side and gripped its handle in both hands, turning sideways as she tiptoed closer, cocking the poker back and getting ready to swing as hard as she possibly could.

She had to take Vaughn out first, and she had to do it fast. Because he was strong and quick and so much bigger than her and if Willow didn't get him out of the way, she'd never get to Eva, never get to make the psycho bitch suffer.

Willow smiled big at the image of spilling the girl's blood. She wanted it to gush from Eva's broken body and form a river. She wanted to bathe it in. Wanted to *taste* it.

Willow didn't just want to end Eva, she wanted to *consume* her. The ultimate fuck-you.

It all happened so fast then.

Willow twisted her torso back as far as she could, bringing to mind the one single golf lesson her father had sent her to at the local country club when she was in sixth grade where the club pro had taught her all about how to generate torque. She flexed her legs and shifted her weight forward again and had just started the downward arc of her swing, hoping to bury the curved point of the poker into that little patch of bald flesh on Vaughn's skull, when two things happened.

First, Willow had forgotten about the flickering firelight behind her, and her shadow reached Vaughn and Eva before she did, looming over them like a black cloud rolling across the night sky. This caused both Vaughn and Eva to tilt their heads back, startled, eyes searching for the cloud's source, their gaze landing on Willow. Second, a firecracker of light from Willow's left. In an immeasurable flash, Willow would swear she saw Eva's eyes go wide in surprise at seeing her standing over them with her arms cocked and loaded and ready to deliver a death blow, and then she'd quickly reached out with her right hand and shoved Vaughn to the side, sending him rolling over onto his hip, half-off the blanket now. Vaughn was too big for somebody Eva's size to simply push away one-handed with such force. But it hadn't been Eva, not really, who'd pushed him. It had been that firecracker, that light, a supercharged burst of ... *energy* ... that seemed to have shot from Eva's hand. A white light that in the orange glow of the fire and the pale iridescence of the moon looked more pure and clean than anything Willow had ever seen.

Willow had already started her swing, using all her strength to propel the steel rod into Vaughn's brain, and in that moment as the fire poker descended toward the boy she'd been so obsessed with for so long, her mind chewed through two rapid conclusions.

One ... whatever dark energy Willow felt pulsing through her right now, the black smoke that plumed into the air from those flames in her mind, Eva's white flash of purity was its antithesis. The antidote to a poison. Willow looked at everything Eva had done today and everything she'd said, everything she'd confided in Willow and all the warnings she'd given, and in a completely surprising acquiescence, Willow had just enough time to think, *I guess she was telling the truth after all.*

Two ... she was now going to miss Vaughn's scar, and his skull entirely.

The hooked point slammed into the side of Vaughn's neck with a meaty *thwack* that sounded like somebody had stabbed a watermelon, catching him just as he was trying to push himself off the ground. His eyes bulged from their sockets and he whistled a scream that was already gurgling with blood. Both his hands reached up and wrapped around the piece of steel stuck in his throat, and Willow dropped the handle, hearing Vaughn's skin and muscle rip and tear as the weight shifted. He cried out again, the sound weaker now, and he fell back to the ground, onto his side, his feet kicking like he was trying to swim away on land.

Willow didn't wait to watch him die, because movement drew her attention to her left again, toward the trees.

Eva was running through the grass, headed for the tree line. She tripped on something and yelled and went down hard, making Willow smile big again. *This place is mine*, she thought. *You aren't welcome here.*

Eva stood back up and started moving again, a little more slowly now. Maybe she'd twisted an ankle or broken a toe. Willow didn't care but was thankful for the delay. Because with Eva nearly halfway to the trees, Willow knew she'd never catch her on foot, no matter how superhuman she felt. But, thankfully, Willow felt like her mind was racing at speeds she'd never imagined possible, kicking open doors to solutions that might have taken Old Willow much longer to pick the locks.

Willow rushed around to the van's driver's door and pulled it open. Found the keys in the cupholder and cranked the engine. She looked out the passenger window and saw that the engine noise had caused Eva to stop again, just long enough to look back over her shoulder. Willow waved, wiggling her fingers, then threw the shifter into Drive and mashed the accelerator to the floor.

The tires spun and slipped in the grass long enough for the rear end to slide, but when they caught purchase, the van shot forward with angry speed. The back hatch was still open, and the cooler flew out, spilling mostly melted ice in a wide arching spray, droplets sizzling as they landed in the fire. Willow flicked on the headlights as she turned the wheel hard to the right, the beams of light sweeping across the yard until Eva was highlighted.

"Gotcha now, bitch!" Willow screamed and found the voice wasn't hers at all. It was deep and gravelly and tasted like cigarettes. But she did not slow down, she stood on the gas pedal with all her weight. Eva was limping toward the trees as fast as she could move, but it wasn't nearly fast enough, and with the van only twenty yards away now, the headlights throwing a giant-sized version of Eva's shadow out in front of her across the trees, Eva must have realized it was all over, she'd never make it.

Eva stopped running. She spun around and held up her

hand, palm up. The universal signal for STOP. Willow saw a faint glow of that white light in Eva's palm, fuzzy, like static on an old television. But it was Eva's eyes that caught Willow off guard. Her eyes cut through the night and the van's windshield and struck Willow in the heart. They carried a message, words echoing inside Willow's mind.

You don't have to—

Willow never stopped. The van struck Eva square-on and the girl flew backward through the air, weightless, instantly broken. Her body slammed into a wide tree trunk and stuck there for a moment, her eyes now lifeless but somehow still staring directly back to Willow. Willow slammed on the brakes and brought the van to a stop just feet away from the trees. She looked away, suddenly feeling very unsettled by Eva's death stare, just a quick glance out the side window and back, but long enough so that when she looked back out the windshield Eva's body had slid down the tree trunk and was now seated, back resting against the tree and legs splayed awkwardly out in front and the chin leaned down against the chest. If not for the blood dripping from her mouth, it might have looked like Eva was only taking a nap.

And then the world went quiet.

The buzzing in Willow's ears stopped, and all the electric pulsing of that pent-up energy inside of her faded away. Her mind felt light and empty, wiped clean like a chalkboard after class was finished for the day. The superhuman strength she'd been so propelled by drained out of her like somebody had pulled the plug, and Willow found her own eyes growing heavy with exhaustion, caught her own chin nodding down to her chest.

Just a quick rest, she thought. *I've earned it.*

With her last bit of strength, her hand feeling heavy and numb, Willow used her thumb and index finger and switched the key to the off position. The van's engine fell silent; Willow slumped back into the seat and closed her eyes.

Just a quick rest.

A rustling noise from up ahead opened her eyes to slits, her vision blurry as she squinted out the windshield, feeling like the real world was more dreamlike than ever.

Something ... diff ... different, her spent and dying mind finally pieced together.

Willow never realized what was different was that Eva's dead body was no longer propped against the tree. It wasn't anywhere at all to be seen. Gone.

The tree limbs and low branches did not so much sway as bend and break and snap as something big lumbered forward, that rustling noise it produced once again reminding Willow of the way the branches had danced against the night sky as she'd stood on the dock and listened to their message.

Willow saw the eye first, as big as a basketball and all a dull emerald green that was beautiful and terrifying as it reflected the moonlight in its glossy surface. Then came the long, multijointed arms, lanky and full of ropy muscles and tendons and covered in what looked like smooth black leather. Each one—and there were *several*, too many for poor, tired Willow to count—were tipped with a sharp talon, as big as a butcher's knife.

Willow closed her eyes again and lowered her chin to her

chest, a satisfied grin on her lips. Because she recognized that eye and those talons, and she understood that her purpose had been fulfilled. The thing from the woods was proud of her, she had seen it in that big green eye that had somehow been looking everywhere at once but also solely focused in on her.

And she could feel it too. The last thing Willow would ever feel.

Love.

It loves me, Willow thought, just as she felt the van rock to the side and heard the door get ripped open. *It loves what I've done.*

Blackness was drowning her now, pulling her deep under. She wished she could find the strength to lift her head and look into the thing's big, beautiful eye one more time so she could tell it she loved it too. Would always love it. For now and all eternity.

But she couldn't.

The talon was quick and painless.

Willow was gone.

LANDLORDS
(INTERLUDE)

Don't ask how long they've been here, because you won't get an answer.

Not because they can't speak—they *can* speak, every language spoken across the history of mankind—or because they don't know, but because for them time does not exist, and therefore cannot be measured. Time is a construct that humans developed because they are simple-minded creatures trapped inside a limited understanding of the Universe. To function, mankind enforced the linear, the scheduled, the ordered.

But the Universe is none of those things.

The Universe is a tangle of spiderwebs, intermingled meshes of realities and outcomes existing simultaneously on the multidimensional plane of the cosmos.

The Universe is what humans call chaos.

But even in the chaotic nonorder of these multiple dimensions, there are anomalies. Patterns that can be observed by those with the sight, those with the power.

Those in control.

Those in control on *both* sides of the great divide.

The Darkness and the Light.

The house is one of these anomalies. A structure constructed at the statistically unlikely intersection of dimensional paths, an overlapping of existences that are progressing both independently and simultaneously. Wholly their own, but also bleeding over into the others, while the others bleed into them. A transfusion of truths.

This overlapping of dimensions continued to grow, fresh realities spawning day by day, stacking higher and higher, and those in power began to notice something else. A great energy building, growing stronger with each additional existence until it began to burn with a bright intensity that shook and rumbled through the Universe like an apocalyptic warning, a volcano about to erupt.

And then one day, finally, it did. But the destruction was not as feared, was not a shattering of these realities and a severing of the paths, but instead a small tear in the plane, a gateway to a new dimension comprised of all of those before it, a playground of possibility and opportunity and, most importantly, *control*.

Whoever controlled this new dimension would also control all those that came before it and came after it as the layers continued to stack and the Universe refused to slow in its unwavering, infinite expansion.

A great war was waged, the Light and the Darkness battling for control of this new and dangerous anomaly.

The Darkness won.

Evil blackened the worlds within the tear, turning the

bright, burning energy into thick, impenetrable storm clouds of despair. And at the center of it all, where the clouds were the darkest, there was always the house, seeped in and oozing with Evil to the point that it served as a beacon, a magnet whose field reached far and wide and found those prone to Darkness, those with black spots already festering in their hearts and minds, and it pulled them in, propelled them to the house where they would face their Evil head-on, let it break them down, destroy them. Let them be sacrificed, so their Evil could be consumed.

And the Darkness would grow stronger.

Through it all, the LandLORDS were always watching, feeling the immense euphoria of each new death, each new devastation. They played their part, guiding and aligning when necessary. Reaching inside the minds of the vulnerable, plucking the right strings to create the chord that would send their sacrifice over the edge.

When the end did inevitably come—because the LandLORDS had never failed, they were far too powerful—they would emerge from their hiding in the shadows and watch as the sparkling black energy from the Evil that had been trapped inside their guests (*everyone* had it inside them, if only a little taste) began to release itself into the air, make its way back into the Universe. Full circle. Ashes to ashes, dust to dust. The LandLORDS would lap up this ethereal nectar with poisoned tongues, letting it renew and refresh them.

But they did not consume it all. They let the Universe have its portion, paying their tithes, strengthening their control and further fortifying their defenses against the Light. And the rest ... they collected this energy and compressed it, changed its state of matter to something more tangible, more earthlike. The result, a treat for the guests, was a pile of sparkling black crystals that looked very much like what the humans called ... *coffee*.

With a job done, the LandLORDS would *clean up*—meaning they would shift themselves to another dimension, another reality. The house was always there, of course. New, yet still the same. Relics of a million or more lifetimes trapped within its walls, littering its land, haunting its pond.

The LandLORDS would slither back into the shadows and wait.

The house always found a new guest.

DECLAN
III

1

Willow was gone.

Declan read the final words of Willow's story and then shivered, feeling as though a ghost was tiptoeing up his spine. The chill shook him, startling him and freeing his mind from the book's pages. He looked up from the book and sucked in a deep breath, the air icy in his throat, and the world around him came rushing back, his own reality solidifying once more. This was a feeling Declan was familiar with, one he usually enjoyed experiencing—that emerging-from-a-dream feeling he would get after spending hours buried in a good book, lost in its world, walking side by side with its characters, and then pulling himself free and looking up and remembering where he was, *who* he was, because for a while he had simply forgotten.

This time, when his world took shape around him again, Declan found that the feeling was different. Different ... but also the same. He looked down at his feet, which were still dangling only an inch or so above the water's surface as his legs swung gently back and forth over the edge of the dock, and he thought, *Those are my feet. But they also aren't my feet.*

And that was the way it *all* felt. His, but also not his.

A cold breeze swooped over the treetops, rustling branches and whistling softly across the pond. Declan's head swiveled to his left, eyeing the tree line, his imagination still freshly seared with the image of Willow slumped in the driver's seat of Vaughn's van while the grotesque beast lumbered from the woods.

Declan shivered again, felt a lump of fear rise in his throat as his heart suddenly started pounding in his chest.

And then he laughed, embarrassed. He usually didn't get spooked by horror novels or movies, so he was surprised to find himself having such a visceral reaction to the tale he'd just finished. He'd done something similar with the previous story, the one about Ivan and his down-on-their-luck siblings, when he'd have sworn he'd seen the black Dodge Charger parked outside the back door.

He could feel that fuzziness clouding his mind, his thoughts beginning to scramble again, but then a voice sliced through the haze.

Leave. Leave before it's too—

There was a screech in Declan's mind and the voice was silenced, like a needle being ripped from a spinning record. As the underlying buzz began to dominate his thoughts once more, Declan realized he had recognized that voice.

It was Eva.

And, no, he wasn't so far gone as to think that Eva was actually *real* and somehow talking to him, what ... telepathically? But the voice he'd heard in his head was the same voice that Declan had used in his mind when reading Eva's dialogue in the story. The voice that had accompanied the face Declan had conjured for her character.

And he'd seen it, hadn't he? Just now, when his made-up Eva voice had cut through the static, Declan had caught a glimpse of her face in his imagination once more.

Declan stood on the dock, the darkness almost fully swallowing the yard now, the house becoming nothing more than a hulking shape in the shadows, and tried to chase the feeling that something felt very ... wrong. Tried to chase it so he could grab ahold of it and see where it led and maybe try and understand why he was suddenly unsure of ... *anything.*

But he never caught it. Instead, the simplest answer reached him, the excuse he'd used all day long.

Tired, Declan thought. *I'm fucking exhausted. Can't think straight to save my life.*

He tucked the book under his arm and walked back to the house, hunching against the cold that had accompanied the dark, thinking he might just turn in for the night. Give his mind the rest it deserved. But as he reached the back door and turned the knob, he felt the craving and decided maybe he'd stay up a little longer.

He filled the kettle and lit the stove and waited for the water to boil so he could enjoy one more cup of coffee, thinking the caffeine might help burn away some of the cobwebs obscuring his thoughts.

The stuff was just so *damn* good.

2

Declan had set the black book down on the kitchen table and found himself stuck, standing in place and staring at the cover, which was now blank once again, Willow's name gone.

Willow was gone, Declan thought and realized there was something about Willow's story that was hovering just above his reach. Something about the tale that had affected him and was *staying* with him more than any of the blood or the monsters in the woods. He'd felt the pull of the moment when he'd read the words, his consciousness trying to get his attention, drag him back to reality to discuss. But Declan had been too engrossed in the story, too wrapped up in the pages. He'd been rooting for Willow, wanting her to get the guy, and by the time she had grabbed the fire poker and started her rampage, Declan found that he'd been rooting for her even more.

Kill them all, he remembered himself thinking as he'd turned the pages. *They don't deserve you.*

"Wait." Declan looked away from the book, squinted in the nearly dark kitchen, the gentle blue and white flames from the stove's burner flickering in the corner of one eye. "Did I want her to kill them?"

He asked, but nobody answered. Again, he didn't feel right. The thought didn't feel like him. He remembered rooting for Willow, empathizing with her, even, but there was another part of him that seemed to feel like he'd gotten frustrated with her as the story went on. Wondered why she'd grown so increasingly unstable and—

A shrill scream from the kettle derailed his thoughts, steam billowing in a ghostly cloud overtop the stove. Declan was overcome with excitement, eager to pour his next cup, a junkie anticipating his next hit. He spooned four heaping scoops into his mug, or was it only two? He couldn't remember. Decided to put two more in, just in case. Better to make it too strong than too weak.

If I wanted weak coffee, I'd just drink hot tea!

He giggled to himself as he poured in the water and stirred, and as the coffee grounds began to dissolve, Declan would have sworn they'd been sparkling as they swirled, creating a galaxy of stars in his mug.

His phone chirped in his pocket, and he again felt silly when he jumped, another lump in his throat and a sputter of his heart. But then the quick jolt of fear was replaced with simultaneous elation and worry.

Norah! The thought of her brought a smile to his face and flash of warmth in his stomach.

But then...

Norah! Knox! Oh my God, I forgot all about them!

It was true. He'd fallen into such a trance out on the dock, with his mug of coffee and the crisp, chilled air, and the book, that he'd completely forgotten about his family, about their flight. He felt such shame wash over him as he pulled his phone free from his pocket. *Are they alright? Did the plane land on time? Are they lost? Wait ... was I supposed to pick them up at the airport? Why can't I remember anything! I'm the worst! They deserve so much better than me.*

He checked his phone screen, already anticipating angry texts or voice mails from Norah. The way the cell reception seemed to be so spotty out here, he had a nightmare idea that she might have been trying to call or text him all day to no avail, only for him to get hit with a deluge of her anger all at once.

But there were no missed calls. No voice mails or text messages. The notification on his phone was a low-battery warning.

Fuck.

Declan stared at his phone's lock screen. The picture was one of his favorites. It was of him and Norah out to dinner to celebrate the sale of his first book. They were younger then, and—*happier, Deck. You were happier*—looked so carefree. Invincible. Selling that first book had felt like the beginning of something grand, something wondrous and elegant and full of promise. The promise of a future full of life and love and—

My book...

That nagging thought that had been dangling just out of reach, the thing about Willow's tragic story that had wormed its way into him, became whole and clear.

"She was reading *my* book," Declan said into his coffee, which he didn't even remember picking up and bringing to his lips. He took a sip, felt the delicious heat slide down his throat. Yes, he recalled the scene perfectly now. When the group had been eating their hot dogs by the fire, Eva and Cesca had started discussing an English class and Eva had shown what book she'd been reading for an assignment and it had been—

"A Family History of Skulls..." Declan spoke the words that he'd spoken a thousand times before. The title of the book that was supposed to have changed his life. Changed *their* lives. "Eva said she'd seen me in the window, looking out."

Declan took another sip of coffee and looked around the kitchen, then he closed his eyes and let his mind float down the hallway and into the living room. Saw the piece of a burnt US bill in the fireplace that he'd found earlier. *A hundred-dollar bill.* Then he floated up, through the ceiling and into the bedroom above, where in the corner sat a lonely bottle of rum, almost empty.

Impossible, he thought. He opened his eyes again and looked over toward the black book on the kitchen table. *It's not real. It's only a story. Somebody made it all up and...*

Declan felt another smile spread across his face, bigger and bigger until he couldn't help it any longer and he burst out in laughter.

Genius! Declan thought. His body shook with his laughter and some of the coffee sloshed over the brim of his mug and burned his hand, but Declan never felt it. He was too thrilled by what he'd realized. Too excited. Because the truth—and it *had* to be the truth, because it was the only thing that made any sense at all—was so impressive and so flattering Declan felt downright giddy.

Earlier, after he'd finished reading the Ivan story, Declan realized that whoever had written the story had clearly used this house as inspiration and setting. Declan had briefly entertained the idea that maybe the book's unknown author had actually been the house's previous owner. But now,

Declan was certain that was exactly the case. Not only had Declan and Norah bought their new home from another writer—a very gifted one at that—but the person had obviously recognized Declan's name and must have decided to write these stories and then stage the house with these little props as a sort of, what, welcome gift?

Declan laughed again. Loved it. What a fun idea. When Norah got here, Declan was going to have to get her to show him the documents online so he could get the home's seller's name and information so he could reach out and say *Well done!*

Two currents of emotion began to form great swells in Declan's gut. One was pride. He took another sip of coffee and leaned against the old kitchen counter and for a moment allowed himself to revel in the fact that this other author had done all this for him. Because, the way Declan figured, if the other author had recognized Declan's name and had not enjoyed or appreciated Declan's work, none of this would have happened. There would be no book, no ruse. Hell, maybe Declan would have found a charred copy of his own book in the fireplace instead.

No, the other author must have respected Declan's writing, and this thought almost allowed Declan to feel a surge of happiness stronger than he'd felt in a very long time.

The second emotion was one that Declan had been secretly afraid that he might never feel again, and it quickly squashed the impending happiness. Though, in its own way, it was a better feeling.

Declan felt *inspired*.

3

Call it fate, destiny, serendipity, or whatever the hell you wanted to call it—all of those words accompanied the cliché phrase *Everything happens for a reason.* But cliché or not, for the first time in his life, Declan Scheider felt power and truth in those words, in that phrase. After all his recent struggles, all his personal and professional issues that had plagued him as of late to the point that he genuinely feared there would never be any light at the end of his tunnel, would never be able to become the husband and father his wife and newborn son deserved, Declan swam in warm waters of relief as he realized that it had all been building to this.

The house.

A place where he'd finally break down those walls of his writer's block and free his trapped imagination and be able to sit down at a computer again and write the words that once upon a time had flowed so freely from his fingertips. This place had made him feel different from the moment he woke this morning, and it wasn't until the moment in the kitchen as he drank his mug of coffee and stared at the black book on the kitchen table and let the whole day sink into him did he finally realize what that feeling really was, and why it had felt so foreign.

Declan felt *alive*.

Felt as though he'd just awakened from a deep hibernation within himself, a coma patient fluttering their eyes open after months of unresponsiveness. His mind raced, the story and the words crowding his thoughts until it was standing room only, and then kept coming. Pushing and shoving, starting fights. Declan couldn't keep those words inside him any longer. Had to let them out before his head exploded.

A pulsing golden glow lit up the kitchen. Declan's eyes fell to the kitchen table, the source of the light. Found that the golden light was burning brightest in a streak across the book's front cover, a jagged neon scribble. Declan walked forward, eyes never leaving the book, even as he stood directly over the table and peered down into that pulsing golden light and stared directly into it, blinding himself, burning away everything but the word that was written there, the word that was written in gold.

DECLAN

"I'm here," Declan said, nodding his head up and down over and over, everything finally making sense. "I'm ready."

It had been about the book all along. It had been waiting for Declan to understand, waiting for him to do the exact thing he'd been brought here for.

Ivan ... Willow ... they'd told their stories. Now it was time for Declan to tell his.

Declan reached out and touched his finger to the book. The golden light flashed a brilliant burst of color, a rainbow grenade, and then everything went dark.

I need a pen! Declan thought, frantic. His entire being consumed with performing no other task except to write. Tell his story. Do what he was meant to do. The only thing he'd ever been meant to do.

In my bag. I have a pen in my bag! He turned around fast, more coffee splashing his hand and shoes, and bumped his knee hard against the table. In response, Declan heard the quick, gentle thud of something from atop the table, and he knew instantly what the sound had been. The book had opened itself, waiting for him to fill its pages.

"I'm trying!" Declan yelled. He rushed across the floor to the light switch near the hall and flicked it up. Nothing happened. "*Shit! I never did call the power company!*"

He still gripped his cell in the hand not holding his coffee, and he fumbled with the screen until he was able to turn on the flashlight, a light that seemed very ho-hum compared to the golden light that had been cast by the book but got the job done well enough. He found his satchel and slipped a pen from the side pouch, a cheap ballpoint he had purchased in a pack of twenty from the drugstore, nothing special, certainly not worthy of the book's pages, not worthy of his story. But much like his phone's flashlight, it would get the job done well enough.

The tools didn't matter. All that mattered were the words. The *story*.

Declan gulped down the rest of his coffee and set the empty mug on the counter, his heart racing in anticipation, his fingers tingling. He felt electric. He laid his cell phone facedown on the table so that the light shone up toward the ceiling, a tiny lantern at his side. Enough for him to see the blank page that was waiting. He took a seat, slid the book closer to him, hunched over it as if he were meant to protect it, and then touched the pen's tip to the paper.

The words came. Once they started, they refused to stop. Declan told his story with a fervor that he'd never experienced before while writing. The act felt familiar, finally writing again, but also brand-new, as if maybe he'd never actually known how to write before.

Before the house.

His cell phone battery died and the kitchen went pitch black, but still Declan did not stop. He didn't need to see the pages with his eyes. He could feel them reaching inside him, guiding his thoughts, guiding the pen. They were him.

The words came.

4

Declan woke with his face in a puddle of his own drool, the kitchen table hard and unforgiving against his cheek. His eyes fluttered open and then squinted against a morning light that was more white and cold than golden and warm, a harsh slap to the face. He groaned and pushed himself up, the muscles in his back screaming profanities, his legs and one arm asleep, feet tingling as if resting upon needles. His mouth was dry and his tongue felt rough across his lips, his teeth fuzzy. Disorientation and confusion wreaked havoc on his just-woken thoughts, and a dull headache pulsed deep behind his eyes, a painful heartbeat at the center of his skull.

He felt like death, but when his eyes found the black book atop the table, the top half of his cheap ink pen sticking out from the closed pages like a bookmark, all the pain and confusion went away and were replaced with the familiar thrill that had overcome him the night before.

My story! Declan stood back from the table and ran his hands through his hair, hardly able to contain his once-again-found excitement. *How much did I write? How* long *did I write?*

The questions flooded in as Declan tried to remember his night. He looked around the kitchen expectantly, like he might find clues that would help fill in the gaps. All he saw was the book with pen sticking out the top, his empty coffee mug, his satchel, and the coffee can and kettle by the stove. All exactly where he remembered them being when he'd been so consumed by his shock of inspiration, his uncontainable and undeniable desire to write, *really* write for the first time in far too long.

By the look of things, Declan hadn't moved a single time after he'd sat at the table, picked up the pen, and gone to work on the pages. He closed his eyes and tried to think, tried to remember anything that had happened after that moment. He came up blank and decided he must have written until he had absolutely exhausted his brain and he'd simply shut down and fallen asleep facefirst on the table. The puddle of drool that glistened in the sunlight coming through the back door's glass indicated he'd apparently slept hard, lost to the world.

But...

Why can't I remember what I wrote?

Declan rubbed the side of his face, felt the scratchy stubble that peppered his cheek. It was true. He remembered sitting down to write, remembered the actual act of putting the tip of the pen to the page, but after that it was all ... dark.

"How could I write for so long and not remember a word of it?" His words sounded quiet in the kitchen, like the house's walls had swallowed them.

What was it even about? he wondered.

He had to piss, and now that his excitement was wearing off again, he felt grogginess begin to creep back in and he thought he should probably make another cup of coffee, but his curiosity overruled them all and Declan sat back down in the chair and slid the book toward him. His name was still etched into the front cover, and as he ran his fingers over the letters, he remembered.

My story...

Me.

Declan smiled, feeling good, thinking that what he was about to read must certainly be the best thing he'd ever written. He didn't know why, but it was just a hunch, an instinct. This book would be his defining work, the story of his that people would talk about for years to come.

Maybe even after he'd died.

Declan opened the book, smoothed down the first page, leaned in, and started to read.

The momentary flit of panic was over, thank God.

It had been brief, lasting only five or six seconds after Declan Scheider had awakened on the floor of the cold bedroom, but the fear and anxiety that had filled his veins and caused his heart to thump hard and painfully in his chest and had made his breath hitch and sputter in choking gasps had been strong enough to send a fear-driven SOS message directly to the front of his mind: You're going to die!

Declan's eyes darted back and forth across the page at such speed his vision blurred, yet he somehow found he could still make out each and every word he'd written in his tiny, scrawled penmanship. He read his story, which really was *his* story, at such a frantic speed he managed a papercut on one thumb as he hastily flipped a page and his mind struggled to understand why he'd written this.

What have I done? Declan managed to think in between the onslaught of his own prose. *Why ... this?*

The tale Declan had told through his scribbled words was nothing but a narrative account of all the time he'd spent in and around the house since he'd awakened yesterday morning. It should have been boring, he realized, especially to him, because he'd actually *lived* it. He didn't need a recap, and certainly not one he'd written himself. But ... it wasn't boring. Something about the story, though completely predictable, also felt fresh, compelling, and ... mysterious. Declan found a deeper element of suspense and intrigue in his last twenty-four hours when reading about the events told in this detailed firsthand account. Somewhere along the line, as the pages continued to turn and the words refused to release their hold on him, Declan found himself completely lost in his own story, compelled to race to the last page to see how the story ended.

Stop it, Deck, he scolded himself. *You know how it ends. It must end with you sitting down to write last night, because that's all the life you'd lived before you started.*

But as Declan reached the part of his story from his time last night in the kitchen where he'd made his last cup of coffee and had turned on his cell phone flashlight and had sat at the table to begin his writing, he felt a stone of uneasiness drop into his stomach, causing ripples of sudden, unexpected and unexplainable dread.

Because the story did not end there.

Declan read the scene where he'd awakened in the kitchen, had felt his dry mouth and rough tongue and tense back muscles. He read the moment where he remembered his excitement in starting to write in the book, how he was sure it would be his best work.

He read about himself getting confused about reading about himself getting confused.

And then, since the words kept going, his own phantom consciousness somehow laid out on the page bare for all to see, to give him the answers to questions he'd yet learned he needed to ask, Declan kept reading.

His heart pounded in his chest as he finished the last few pages, his stomach turning sour, his head shaking back and forth—*No no no no*—as the words began to run out.

He reached the end.

Then he screamed.

5

What have I done?

Those words again, parading across his mind. Only now Declan stood outside, behind the U-Haul that he'd driven all those long hours to get here, staring at the latch for the big rollup door. Not quite ready to reach out and touch it.

The ground was covered in a light dusting of white. It had snowed last night, sometime after he'd fallen asleep, or maybe even while he'd been nose-deep in the pages of that terrible book, filling those pages with his own disgusting words. Words that could not be true...

Could they?

The cold air nipped at his collar, and snow flurries started to fall to the ground in a slow yet mesmerizing dance. It should have been beautiful. *Would* have been beautiful ... if not for the ugly truth that Declan knew he was now about to face. The ugly truth that would obliterate all the happiness he had ever experienced, like a galactic supernova of his heart and his soul.

Declan found that he wasn't afraid. Just like the cold was seeping into his bones, acceptance had found a home inside him too. It was not fear that kept him from reaching for the handle of the big rollup door. Declan only wanted to breathe a little longer, soak in the last few seconds before his world came to an end. He wanted to relish being alive for as long as possible, even though he now understood that inside he'd been dead all along.

He took a breath of the cold, clean air, and as he reached for the handle, tears streaked down his face as all his repressed memories were unlocked and allowed out into the open space of his mind. He groaned as his actions replayed themselves in his thoughts, showed him the monster he'd let himself become. The terrible thing he'd ended up doing.

He gripped the metal handle in his palm, its surface icy cold, and then Declan cried out, "I'm so sorry!" as he jerked the handle up, freeing the latch, and pushed the door up on its track.

Declan sobbed when he saw what was in the back of the truck. There was no furniture. No boxes. Nothing at all, except death.

6

Declan had gotten it all wrong.

He'd thought the house was their new beginning, their fresh start. In reality, it was his end.

My story is over, Declan thought, still a writer in his heart, right up until his final moments.

He stepped up to the edge of the dock and stopped with the toes of his sneakers an inch over the water. When he looked down into the water, he knew exactly what he'd find.

The blackened and decaying hands were waiting, reaching through the murkiness for him, waving him in, letting him know the water was just fine. Declan leaned down and stared harder, peering deeper into the black until he found what he was looking for.

He saw his own face.

Not his reflection in the water's surface, but a swollen, rotting corpse visible between those beckoning hands. Declan's hands.

The face in the water was the true version of himself, the monster he'd become. It'd been waiting there all along, just beneath the surface.

Declan stepped off the dock, and the hands pulled him home.

EPILOGUE

1

Harvey Wheeler knew this mountain road as well as he knew the curves of his wife's body. Just as his hands had repeatedly explored and enjoyed every inch of Melinda's skin over the course of their thirty-year marriage, Harvey had made this drive up one side of the mountain pass and down the other nearly as many times. He'd moved here right out of high school. He and his buddy Chucky Winston had packed up and headed out of their hometown because they'd heard there was work to be had at the lumberyard. Good-paying work. They'd both gotten hired on at the age of eighteen, and at age nineteen Chucky had been crushed to death in a freak accident involving a dropped pallet of two-by-fours and a hungover crane operator. Harvey had quit the very next day.

He joined the county sheriff's office a month later, had

made a good career of it—good enough to provide the food and the roof and the occasional vacation for Melinda and the girls without ever having to have the bill collectors come calling—and now was counting down his last year before retirement. Full pension.

He knew these roads well, *all* of them. Which was why he had been sitting stopped in the middle of the road, foot on the brake, eyes locked onto the small opening in the trees on this particular mountain road with nothing but mistrust, for nearly two full minutes.

"Yo, are you going to drive or what?"

Harvey pulled his gaze away from the road and turned his head slowly to look at his partner.

Ha. *Partner.* Austin Shoreman was fresh out of training and only two weeks on the job. He was young and strong and handsome and a complete fucking asshole, in Harvey's not-so-humble opinion. Arrogant and borderline intolerable.

When Harvey had asked his longtime pal, Sheriff Gil Haney, why he'd decided to stick Austin with Harvey, Gil had laughed and said, "Because maybe you can straighten his ass out!"

Harvey didn't want to straighten anybody out. Didn't want to babysit. He wanted to drink coffee and drive around and do as little as possible for the next seven months until the pension came.

"You can call me *Harvey*, or *sir*, or *Deputy Wheeler*," Harvey said to Austin, narrowing his eyes at the boy. "What you cannot call me is *yo*. Understood? You wear a badge, you show respect to the citizens of the county, *and* to your peers.

Especially your elders. Which in your case is just about everybody. Got it?"

Harvey saw the flash in Austin's eyes, a twitch of anger. The kid wanted to mouth off, wanted to tell Harvey to fuck off, Harvey could see that much. Part of Harvey almost wished the kid would. It would give Harvey an excuse to kick the kid out of the cruiser and let him walk back to town. Gil wouldn't fire him for a little stunt like that, not after all these years.

Austin, apparently thinking better of saying anything too disrespectful, regardless of what vile thoughts might be loaded onto his tongue, simply nodded and then said, "What are we waiting for, *Harvey*?"

Harvey took a deep breath and then turned his attention back to the road, pointed to the opening in the trees. "That road shouldn't be there."

This must have been too bizarre a statement for even Austin to come up with a snarky retort. All he offered was, "Uh, what do you mean? It's, like, *there*, isn't it?"

Harvey sighed. "Yes, I can see it's there. What I'm telling you is it's ... it's never been there before, okay? I was driving these roads before you were even born, and I'm telling you, *that* road is new. And I don't know much about construction or civil engineering, but I'm pretty damn confident roads don't pop up overnight like weeds." He pointed to the GPS unit mounted low on the dash, in which Harvey himself had punched in the coordinates the rental company had provided. Their destination was a little blue dot lost in a sea of green that represented the forest. "Look," he added. "GPS isn't showing it either."

The air conditioner was on in the cruiser, working to combat the heat of a late-summer morning. The hum of the fans and the steady purr of the engine filled the silence between the two men for another minute, and in that time Harvey thought maybe the kid understood, maybe he believed him.

Turned out, Austin must have been mulling over what the potential consequences might be for what he was about to say next and decided they wouldn't be severe. "You know those things aren't always accurate, and with all due respect, *sir*, to me that sounds like maybe you're getting a bit senile." Then, "You want me to drive? I mean, if you're too scared to do the job, just say so. I'm sure everyone back at the station will understand. When they ask us if we found the missing U-Haul, or any trace of the couple ... what were their names?"

Automatically, Harvey said, "Declan and Norah Scheider."

Harvey always read every report twice. Front, back and sideways. He memorized every detail.

"Right," Austin said. "When they ask if we found the U-Haul or the Scheiders, I'll tell them no because old Harvey got spooked by an old gravel path in the trees. I'm sure you and all the elders can have a good laugh over that one, right?"

After briefly fantasizing about breaking the kid's nose, Harvey hated himself for thinking the kid was right. They had a job to do, and if Harvey let fear stop him from doing it, then despite all his years of experience, he'd be just as worthless as Austin.

Fighting all his instinct and urges and warning bells in

his head, Harvey eased off the brake and drove the car onto the gravel road, into the cover of the trees.

2

To distract his mind from just how *off* the whole thing felt—Harvey's hackles raising even more the deeper he drove the cruiser into the trees—Harvey occupied himself with the details from the report, the reason he and the little shithead Austin were there in the first place.

The case that had been sent to them from a midsized police department a couple states over hadn't grown cold, exactly, but it was certainly cooling off. All the leads had dried up, and aside from the initial crime scene and the testimony of a neighbor and psychiatrist, there wasn't much to go on.

Six months ago, Declan Scheider, thirty-one, and his wife, Norah, twenty-nine, had gone missing. So had the U-Haul their neighbor, Gary Atwood, had just rented in order to pack up all his elderly mother's belongings after moving the woman into an assisted living facility. When Gary had awakened to find his U-Haul missing, he had begun the short walk next door to ask Declan if he had seen or heard anything in the night but had stopped short when he'd seen the dried trail of blood that began at the end of his driveway. Alarmed more than curious, Gary had followed the blood trail directly to the Scheiders' front door. He'd called for Declan and Norah several times and, upon receiving no answer, had phoned the police without stepping foot inside the home.

Harvey had looked at the few crime scene photos that

had come along with the report. The photo of the queen-sized bed in the master bedroom was the most telling. One side of the bed was completely undisturbed, the comforter tight, the pillows stacked neatly. The other side was a bloodbath, the covers flipped down, the pillows soaking in a crimson pool.

"I knew he'd been struggling," Gary told the police. "I think they were in a bit of pinch financially, but most of all, Deck had gotten so afraid of being a dad. He was convinced he'd fail, that his son would be born and would hate him. I ... I had no idea he was hurting this badly."

Norah had been five months pregnant with the couple's first child. A baby boy they had decided to name Knox.

The keys to the U-Haul had been left tucked under the sun visor, with the doors unlocked. It was a safe neighborhood, after all, and the U-Haul itself was empty. Gary told the police he'd never even thought twice about it.

When police had spoken to the psychiatrist that Declan Scheider had been seeing off and on for the better part of eight years, a Dr. Patricia Pillsman, the doctor had appeared deeply saddened to learn of the events, as would any human being with a heart, and had shaken her head and looked down at the ground for a moment before again looking the interviewing officer in the eye and saying, "I tried so hard to help him. But what makes it worse is I truly believe he was trying too. Sometimes the demons are just too powerful." She paused here, looked down to the ground again, and then met the interviewing officer's eyes with an intensity that demanded attention. "Don't for a moment think that Evil isn't real. It is very real, and very alive in this world."

The stolen U-Haul had turned out to be the spark that had relit the case. It had been equipped with a GPS tracker, God bless technology, and the rental company had been able to track the vehicle's course across state lines, covering almost two hundred miles, before the signal had simply died. The police investigated the last known reported location the signal had transmitted, which had been right off an interstate exit ramp, but all they'd found was a trickle of tired traffic and a run-down gas station. The working theory was Declan had figured out how to disable the device, or in a truly unfortunate episode of coincidental timing, the unit had simply failed. It did happen from time to time, the rental company admitted.

But then, just two days ago, the rental company alerted the police that after all these months the tracker had come back online. No rhyme or reason or explanation. They forwarded the coordinates to them, and the police department contacted the closest law enforcement agency they could find within range of the U-Haul's new location. The new coordinates were only a handful of miles from where the signal had been lost initially, somewhere in the middle of a mountain that served as a barrier between two small towns.

The report had landed on Harvey's desk, and an hour later he and Austin were on the road.

The trees parted and the sun flared against the cruiser's windshield as Harvey drove from beneath the canopy of limbs and leaves.

"Fuck, there it is," Austin said from the passenger seat. The first words the kid had spoken since they'd driven onto the gravel road that should not exist.

There it is, indeed.

The U-Haul was parked in front of an old farmhouse that something inside of Harvey told him had absolutely no business being there. The back of the U-Haul was open, and even as they were still thirty or so yards away, Harvey could see the body.

3

The smell was atrocious, and while Austin stood off to the side, puking in the grass like the little pussy he was, Harvey used his forearm to wipe sweat from his brow and steeled his stomach against the stench as he looked into the back of the U-Haul and discovered what he could only assume was what was left of Norah Scheider's body. He paid particular attention to the gaping slash across the corpse's throat, and his mind flashed back to the crime scene photo, to that crimson pool beneath the pillows.

With a growing lump of sadness in his gut, one that mixed with Harvey's own incomprehension when it came to just how evil humans could be to one another, to the ones they *loved*, he let his eyes slide from Norah's wounded neck and down to her belly.

Knox. I'm so sorry, little one.

The psychiatrist's quote came back to him, carrying such a sickening truth. *"Don't for a moment think that Evil isn't real. It is very real, and very alive in this world."*

"Radio back and tell dispatch we found the truck. And one body."

Austin stood and wiped his mouth on his sleeve. Nodded

and dashed back to the cruiser on wobbly legs. Harvey stepped to the side and looked around the U-Haul, staring at the house. The house stared back, and Harvey felt a shiver cut through the summer heat and find his spine. He felt exposed, examined.

"Won't work," Austin's voice startled him, and Harvey spun around to see the kid standing a few feet back, making a concerted effort to keep the opened back of the truck out of his line of sight.

"What?"

"The radio won't work. It's all static and squeals."

Harvey didn't like that. Didn't like it one bit. But still...

He had a job to do.

"I'm going to check inside," he said. "Think you can go around and make sure nobody runs out the back?"

To his credit, Austin nodded and headed toward the house, sliding around to the side, hand resting gently atop his pistol in its holster.

Harvey reached the front door and knew he should knock. Knew he should announce himself before entering. But he also knew it wouldn't make any difference. The nagging feeling of mistrust and anxiousness and unease he'd felt the moment he'd laid his eyes on the beginning of that gravel road had only further intensified in strength, and right now Harvey knew nothing about this place was as it was supposed to be. He wasn't sure what he was going to find inside the house, but he was certain it wasn't going to be Declan Scheider.

He gripped the doorknob, twisted it, and pushed the door open.

The inside of the house was impossibly cold, and where the cool air should have been a pleasant reprieve from the outdoor heat, it only made Harvey uncomfortable. It felt unnatural, overpowering. Like a dessert that was so sweet you couldn't bring yourself to finish it all.

To his left he found an empty living room full of dust and cobwebs and an ugly green couch that might have once been emerald but now barely qualified as dull pea soup, even in the sunlight. To his right, a dining room was equally desperate. He gave both these rooms just a cursory glance, seeing nothing and nobody that interested him, all while he tried to push down a new feeling in his gut, a tug forward, like somebody had gotten a hook into him and was reeling him in.

He knew whatever he was going to find here lay deeper in the house, down the hallway just inside the front door.

"Sheriff's department!" Harvey called out as he walked, if for no other reason than to hear something other than the house's unnerving silence. "If you're here, please make yourself known!"

Of course, there was no answer.

Harvey reached the end of the hallway and found himself in the kitchen, just as a face appeared through the glass of the back door. Austin, reaching the back of the house at the same time Harvey had. Harvey looked once to the kid, and then down to the other thing that had caught his eye, the thing he knew had been what had reached inside of him and pulled him deeper into the house, into the kitchen.

Senile. He heard Austin's voice in his head.

No. I'm not.

Atop the wooden kitchen table, bathed in a stream of

sunlight, sat what Harvey first mistook for an old leather-bound Bible. He stepped closer, leaned down to get a better look. Read the word that gold letters spelled out across the front.

Felt a wave of fresh, deeper fear.

Harvey heard the back door open on near-silent hinges, then listened as Austin's footsteps came closer. The kid's body blocked the sunlight, throwing the book into shadow.

Which is where it belongs, Harvey thought. *It's where it came from.*

"What's that?" Austin asked, a little bravado back in his voice.

Harvey took a deep breath to clear his head, filled his lungs with cold air that carried a faint scent of mildew and something mildly metallic. Then he looked up and met Austin's eyes. "I don't know," he said. "But it's got your name on it."

Author's Note

THE END HOUSE is the first stand-alone novel I've written in several years, and it was a blast to write. It started with a mental image I couldn't shake, that of a writer all alone in an old house, roaming the halls, drinking coffee, and occasionally sitting at a desk to work on a book. I wanted to know why he was there, and I wanted to know what he was working on. Somehow, in that magic way stories tend to manifest themselves, THE END HOUSE was the result. I hope like hell you enjoyed it, and if you did, and you have a few seconds to spare, I'd greatly appreciate it if you could leave a review. They really do help.

I mentioned this novel was my first stand-alone in quite some time, and while that's true, the hero from my main series couldn't help but make an appearance. Because you see, if anybody knows about things that lurk in the shadows and what dangers the Universe is hiding from us normal folk, it's that guy named Lance that poor Eva saw at her

AUTHOR'S NOTE

cousin's basketball game. And Eva was right, Lance is very powerful. So powerful, in fact, the Darkness (those who the LandLORDS serve) want him gone for good.

If you like supernatural suspense and mystery, you'll probably enjoy meeting Lance Brody. There's currently 7 books in the series, all available in ebook, paperback, and audio, and if you're interested you can get a free Lance Brody ebook short story and the audiobook of the prequel novella as a thank you for signing up for my author newsletter. You can find the sign-up link below:

https://mrobertsonjr.com/newsletter-sign-up/

I also want to take this time to thank some very special people—my Patreon members! Your continued support and encouragement means more than you'll ever know. So ... thank you to:

Cesca, Chris Cool, Deana Harper, Debra Kowalski, Diane Benson, Diane Porter, Judi Mickelson, Karin Anderson, Kathy Oudinot, Lisa Fazalare, Lorraine Meyer, Lynette Stone, Marilyn Aiken, Martha Gilmore, Mike Gagliardi, Rebecca Curry, Robert Bray, Tami, and Tanya Wolf. — You guys rock!

Alright, I think that's all for now. As always, thank you so much for reading. Until the next book...

-Michael Robertson, Jr.

For all the latest info, including release dates, giveaways, and special events, sign up for the Michael Robertson, Jr. VIP Readers List. As a Thank You, you'll also receive a FREE audiobook and ebook. (He promises to never spam you!)

http://mrobertsonjr.com/newsletter-sign-up

You can also check out Midnight Coffee — my weekly blog where I also publish the occasional short story.

https://mrobertsonjr.substack.com

More from Michael Robertson Jr

LANCE BRODY SERIES

Dark Choice (Book 7)

Dark Holiday (Book 6)

Dark Rest (Book 5.5 - Short Story)

Dark Woods (Book 5)

Dark Vacancy (Book 4)

Dark Shore (Book 3)

Dark Deception (Book 2.5 - Short Story)

Dark Son (Book 2)

Dark Game (Book 1)

Dark Beginnings (Book 0 - Prequel Novella)

SHIFFY P.I. SERIES

Prey No More (Book 2)

Run No More (Book 1)

OTHER NOVELS

Cedar Ridge

Transit

Rough Draft (A Kindle #1 Horror Bestseller!)

Regret*

Collections

Tormented Thoughts: Tales of Horror

The Teachers' Lounge*

*Writing as Dan Dawkins

Follow On:

Facebook.com/mrobertsonjr

Twitter.com/mrobertsonjr

Instagram.com/mrobertsonjr

Made in United States
North Haven, CT
20 April 2024